PARTED OUT
GRIM REPO FILES

MARK
FASSETT

OTHER BOOKS BY MARK FASSETT

Grim Repo Files
Grim Repo
Parted Out

A Wizard's Work
Shattered
Fragments
* Bloodweave

Lords Of Genova
Questioner's Shadow

Other Novels
The Sacrifice of Mendleson Moony
Minders

Novellas
Dreams of Earth
A Tower Without Doors
Zombies Ate My Mom
Zombies Bought The Farm

* Forthcoming

PARTED OUT
GRIM REPO FILES

MARK FASSETT

RAVENSTAR PRESS
MONROE, WA

Published 2014 by Ravenstar Press
Monroe, WA
http://www.ravenstarpress.com

Interior Design by Ravenstar Press
Cover Design by Ravenstar Press

Images used
© Philcold | Dreamstime.com

ISBN: 978-0692251973

ACKNOWLEDGEMENTS

I'd like to thank the people that helped me through finishing this book: Michael Kingswood, Rebecca M. Senese, David Michael, Kendra Harrington, Jeff Ambrose and Michael Canfield all read and commented on the early drafts. The book would not be the same without their input.

My family, as always, are special and I couldn't do this without their understanding.

••1••

Whenever you transition from one gate to the next, there's always a chance something will go wrong. Power links fail, a fuel monitor decides there's no fuel left, all the desks lose power. It happens. When you make enough jumps, something will eventually crap out.

"Captain," Eddy, my best gunner and currently the duty navigator, said as we recovered from the transition to New Corbi, "we've lost navigation."

She turned her delicate face toward me, her light brown hair pulled back behind her in a tail, and waited for me to give her an order.

I didn't have an order for her, though.

"Just navigation?" I asked. "How do we only lose navigation?"

"I don't know," she said, then turned back to her desk.

"She's right, Captain," said Renaldo without turning to face me. Currently tasked with communications, he was quick to follow up Eddy's diagnosis. With a crew of five, other than myself, they were all trained to do most jobs, and to back each other up. "All other systems and programs check out."

I tried to bring up navigation on my own desk, but it wouldn't come up. It was as if it wasn't there.

I tried to bring up star charts, pinpoint our position. Nothing.

"Well, get us away from this gate," I said. "We don't want to be here when someone else transitions through."

I felt the engines come to life, and the g increase.

At least we could move, but without navigation, we could end up anywhere. A gravity well might have ahold of us and we wouldn't know it until it was too late.

I ran some diagnostics on the system. Normally, I'd have Alice do it, she of the uncompromised intellect and our resident synthetic, but it wasn't her shift, and I wasn't about to wake her.

The diagnostics pinpointed a dead cell in the memory array. Nothing as simple as the navigation software having been moved to inaccessible memory, or deleted. Nothing where we could recover it quickly.

I looked at my screen, then out at the stars. A planet orbited the bright blue ball of energy at the center of the system, a docking facility orbited the planet, and our target was sitting somewhere in that docking facility. The records showed it idle for the last three months, and the delinquent hadn't even been in the system.

Two mil waited for me when I delivered that ship to the bank, and I was stuck in the system with no way of finding the planet or plotting a course to it, even if I could find it.

::2::

PARTED OUT

"Why the hell couldn't it have been gunnery or something we don't need on this trip?" I asked no one in particular.

No one answered me.

The back of my head started to ache like it always does when I'm under too much stress. Seemingly a thousand doctors had tried to fix it. Not a one of them had.

I checked our part inventory to see if we had a replacement memory cell.

We didn't.

Well, maybe we could bring it up from the backup, though I wondered if there would be enough space without the dead memory cell.

I palmed the comm on my desk.

"Alice?"

After a moment, the comm came alive, but she left the video off.

"Captain?"

"I want you to tell me that we have a backup of the navigation software."

"We do, you know that."

"I just wanted to confirm."

"Why?"

"A memory cell failed during the transition, and it appears to have been the one with the navigation software on it."

"That's a problem," Alice said.

"I know. We're stuck if we can't navigate. Can you reload it?"

"No," she said.

"Why not?"

"Captain," she said. "The navigation cell also held all the chart data and everything else necessary for the naviga-

tion software to do its job. All that software and data use up almost the entire cell. There's no other place to put it."

"We can't just delete something else? Maybe move it around?"

"If you can think of something we don't need," she said. "What would you want to get rid of? Communications? Weapons? Maneuvering? Life support?"

I looked out through the screen at the blackness of space, the stars beyond the system, the blue ball of gas at the system's center. We couldn't get rid of any of those things. Communications would leave us unable to talk to anyone, and, despite what I had said aloud, forgoing weapons would leave us defenseless. Out here, within shouting distance of the Fringe, I wasn't going to do that. Maneuvering? Life support? Not a chance.

There was another option that would get us there, and I didn't want to use it. The only other choice was to call for a tow. I wasn't about to do that.

"Shit," I said. "Do we have enough room to back up all the customer data?"

"We back that up all the time," she said.

"No," I said. "*All* the customer data."

"Including the files from Elliot? The ones we're not..."

"Yeah," I said, cutting her off. I didn't want her mentioning the data I'd been collecting about the weapons we had inadvertently learned about on our last repossession job. "Everything."

"I shall see," she said. "If there's room, do you want me to do it?"

"Yes."

::4::

PARTED OUT

Eddy turned and looked at me, blinked, and smiled. If only I was interested like she was. I sometimes think that was the entire reason she signed on. Most ships have a strict anti-fraternization policy. Not mine. I live on the Grim Repo, and I'm not about to deny myself real relationships.

Not that I had any at the moment. My last real relationship blew up in my face, and only recently, I discovered she was a Fed the whole time.

"Captain," Eddy said, "Another ship transitioned in behind us. They are hailing us, asking if we need help."

Eddy must have taken over communications while I was talking with Alice, which meant that Renaldo was running a deeper diagnostic on the ship.

"Tell 'em we don't need any help."

She turned back to her desk.

I wasn't about to take charity when our problems were my own damned fault.

If I hadn't taken that last memory cell—I swear we had another for our secondary computer system—we'd be up and running by now.

I just had to hope there was enough room to back all that data up.

Fortunately, system docking stations never looked at backups unless they suspected criminal activity.

Security on New Corbi shouldn't have any reason to suspect us of criminal activity.

We were there to repo a starship.

··2··

I went to see how Alice was coming along with the backup. I found her in the data room, sitting back, watching dots light up on the screen.

"Still working on it?"

She turned and looked at me, her golden eyes, as always, made it hard to look away.

Not that I would. She was beautiful, perfect lines in her face, her jaw not too prominent, but not shrinking, either. Her skin always looked like it carried a tan, even though she rarely set foot outside of the ship, and I didn't think she was vain enough to spend time artificially tanning.

Her designers had done their work well. If she only had a few more emotions to go with her looks, she would have been perfect, but then, she wouldn't be working on my ship, either.

"Approximately twenty-two minutes left," she said. "You piled a lot of data on that cell in a short amount of time."

I leaned back against the wall, no other chairs being available.

"I guess I did."

"Why are you even looking into that weapon mess? We're through with that job."

I couldn't say. It had become a mild obsession since we left Stantion Prime. Everything had worked out, but the delinquent's claim that he had more of those long-distance-shield-busting weapons stashed somewhere scared me. I knew he probably didn't, but if he did, I wanted to find them, know they were safe. The idea that someone could destroy my ship without my being able to even detect or avoid the shot was disturbing.

"I just have to know," I said.

"If the Feds find out you're looking, they'll want to talk to you," she said. "They'll wonder why, and you'll be left trying to explain how you are not connected with them at all. And I won't help you explain."

"You won't?"

"No. You need to be worried about making money so you can buy parts for the Repo, like spare memory cells."

I smiled, even though I knew she was completely serious.

"That almost sounded like you had an emotion," I said.

"I would not call that an emotion," she said. "I stated a fact."

I watched the screen for a moment.

"It will all fit, right?"

"It should."

"Good. I don't want to lose it."

"You know if they do a scan of the backups, they might find it," she said.

PARTED OUT

"I've already thought of that," I said. "But they have no reason to scan."

"Sitting out here, drifting, gives them every reason to wonder what we are doing out here."

I sighed.

"Fine. Set up an automatic wipe. If they even attempt to access the store that backup is in, delete it."

"It's not in just one store," she said. "It's spread across several."

"You can set that up, right?"

"Of course. It's already done."

Growling at her, as much as I wanted to, wouldn't help anything. She did these things on purpose. Why, I don't know. Maybe she's developed a stilted sort of humor. The designers said it was possible, though unlikely. Most Synths needed far too much stimulation before they could develop emotions to ever make it likely they would. Though, the pleasure Synths—they didn't seem to have trouble.

I had to wonder, though, if those emotions were engineered in.

"Thank you," I said. "Let me know when it's done. I want to get moving."

..3..

Mickey caught up with me in the hallway, his muscle-bound body taking up most of the corridor. No one on this boat could walk past Mickey unless he turned sideways for them.

"Grimm," he said.

"Yeah?"

"When do we get some time off? Ever since that shitpile in Stantion Prime, you've been running us so hard I haven't had time to spend my money."

"That shitpile on Stantion Prime cost us a crapload in credits, and we didn't get even a quarter of it back from the bank."

"I need some station time," he said.

"After this job," I said. "It should put us back in the black, keep the ship from flying apart."

"You promise?"

"Yeah. Two weeks leave when we're done."

A grin spread from ear to ear, and I knew what he was planning to do with it—girls and alcohol, not necessarily in that order.

He turned sideways and let me by.

I also knew I could use a couple weeks, though I wouldn't use them for recreation. I'd use them to do more research.

I continued on up to the bridge, sat down at my desk, and started reviewing my notes on the ship we were going to pick up. It was a task I needed to do, but ever since we arrived in system, I hadn't had the chance.

"Captain." Renaldo said.

I still wasn't going to get a chance, it seemed.

"Renaldo?"

"That ship is hailing us again. Wants to know if we're really all right."

I tapped my desk, brought the communication up on it. I saw its ident for the first time. Salvage Vessel Kestrel. No wonder they wanted to know if we were all right. They were hoping for some free salvage.

I played back the comm.

"Starship Grim Repo, this is Captain Everly of the Kestrel. We've watched you drift now for a couple hours, and we just want to make sure there's not something we could do to help."

Captain Everly looked trim, but his hair hung in thick strands that looked like they hadn't been washed in a week. His nose had obviously been broken in his past, as it took a sharp turn to the left about halfway down his face. The only reason I can imagine he didn't have it reset is that it happened shipboard, and he was too cheap to spring for the procedure.

PARTED OUT

I suppose you could say we were more alike than different, considering he's salvaging something people lost or broke, and I'm repossessing something people haven't paid for, but I have contracts that I respect. Salvagers often just look for empty ships to pillage.

"Captain Everly," I said, "Good to meet you. Thank you for your offer, but we're not in any trouble that we can't fix, I assure you."

The time delay between our ships was miniscule. A few seconds at most. He had hung around instead of going on to New Corbi.

"Good to hear," he said. "If you do need any help, give us a holler. We'll come right back."

"I'll keep that in mind," I said, then shut the comm off. I didn't want to look at his face anymore.

And then I said to Eddy, "Keep an eye on him. If he doesn't leave soon, be ready to power up the weapons. I don't trust him."

"Got it," she said.

"And you, Renaldo..."

"I'll be ready, Captain."

"That's what I like to hear."

I palmed the comm.

"Alice, is it done yet?"

"Nearly."

"Get it done. We need to get moving."

I could have told her to wipe it. Perhaps I should have. But I couldn't stand to lose that data, not so soon after I had acquired it.

Fortunately, Alice commed me about ten minutes later, said the backup was done, the burnt out memory cell replaced, and the Navigation software reloaded.

About time.

The salvage ship had moved off, but slowly, hanging in the area as long as possible. They should have named it Vulture instead of Kestrel. Far more appropriate.

We lit our engines, found our place in the universe, and set our trajectory: New Corbi for a dead simple repossession.

I almost felt good about it. We were moving again, and this repo would put much needed credits into our pockets.

And, more than anything, Mickey's suggestion of a vacation sounded good to me, too. It almost made me wonder what Mira might be doing. She could be anywhere in the galaxy interdicting weapons, chasing drug runners, infiltrating yet another unaware captain's boat and trying to take it from him after becoming his lover like she had done to me.

No. Enough of that. That had happened long ago, and she had explained that it hadn't been personal, except for the lover part.

I wished I could get her out of my mind, but she just kept popping in at inopportune moments.

Alice stepped on to the bridge right at that moment.

"Alice," I said. "I want to go over the repo with you."

She came over to stand by my desk.

We always try to discuss the actual repo before it goes down, usually before we dock. When we haven't done that in the past, things have had a tendency to go wrong. Doesn't mean they always go right. They don't. It's just that they go more wrong when we don't talk first.

And we did it on the bridge so the rest of the crew could listen in. The more they knew, the easier things would be.

"The ship," I said, bringing up the schematic on my desk. "Silon Transport Ship Model 1814. Class III cargo hold, doesn't move terribly fast. Two person minimum crew. Registered name, the Fleeting Star." Alice recited that from memory. She hadn't even looked at the schematic.

I brought up the info we had on the delinquent. He was a chubby man, from the picture, hair kept short. Wore an old time ship captain's uniform in the picture.

"The delinquent," I said, "is William Baty, resident of Acton, CEO of Lightlines Transportation Limited. About twelve months ago, he stopped making payments, and three months ago, docked the Fleeting Star here on New Corbi, and it hasn't moved since."

Alice said nothing, but her eyes studied the man in the image on my desk.

"Do we know about his connections here?" I asked.

PARTED OUT

"He doesn't seem to have any. Inquiries have mostly resulted in questions about when someone will remove the ship from the dock. The unpaid moorage fees are up to a hundred thousand credits, now. He paid the first month."

"And then skipped, so it looks like we won't have to worry about him getting in the way."

"No," Alice said. "All indications are that he's back on Acton and out of funds."

That was new to me.

"When did we hear this?"

"While I was running your backup, I did some more probing."

I looked up at her. I wished I could see past those golden eyes and understand what she was thinking. She had a habit of withholding information until I asked for it. I did not know if it was a flaw in her design, or if she somehow enjoyed it.

"And you didn't think I needed to know this?"

"I knew we would discuss it. Telling you any earlier would not have changed anything."

"He could be filing for bankruptcy right now," I said.

"Would it change anything?" she asked without blinking.

I waited to answer, knowing that, once again, she was right. We could not have got the ship moving any faster than we did.

"No," I said.

"Then what would be the point of me telling you earlier?"

"Because I would like to have known," I said.

I glanced up at Eddy and Renaldo, who were studiously watching their desks. I thought I detected a chuckle out of Renaldo, but it was gone before I could be sure.

"Renaldo," I said.

"Yes, Captain?"

"Do we have clearance with New Corbi station?"

"We do," Renaldo said.

"Get us there quickly," I said.

He poured a little more thrust on.

I hoped it would be enough.

We had to get that ship tagged as repossessed before Mr. Baty filed for bankruptcy. If he did that before we had it, then we lost all right to it, and any pay day we might have had would disappear as if it never existed.

··5··

We followed the salvage ship Vulture in to dock. Not by choice, but they were ahead of us, bigger than us, and apparently had a reservation.

I tried to sleep more than once during the thirty-six hours or so we spent trailing behind the salvage scow, but the worry that we'd get to the station and the ship would be under the protection of a bankruptcy order had me spooked. I slept only fitfully, tossing and turning, getting at most a total of four hours of sleep.

After my third failed attempt to sleep, I finally gave up and went back to the bridge.

"Back so soon, Captain?" Mickey asked.

I had forgotten he was at the controls. My sleep patterns were so screwed up I couldn't tell which shift was which.

"Can't sleep," I said.

"You do this every time," Eddy said.

"I do *not* have this problem every time."

"Every time," she said, and laughed. I liked her laugh.

If only that scow would have hurried, we'd have been on Baty's ship already, maybe even away.

The door to the bridge opened, and Alice stepped through it.

"Good news," she said, "or at least, you'll probably think it's good news."

I spun to face her.

"William Baty appears to have come into some money."

"That's not particularly good news," I said.

And it wasn't. If he got enough, paid the past due on his boat, there was still time for the bank to call off the repo. We'd get a retainer fee, but it wouldn't compare to what we'd get for bringing back the boat.

"Oh, it is if it's not enough to pay his debt to the bank, but is probably enough to keep him from filing for bankruptcy in the next forty-eight hours."

"How much?"

"Fifty-thousand," she said.

A weight lifted off me. It wasn't even enough to pay the docking fees, but it was better than him having an empty bank account. I don't like it when the delinquents feel desperate. Things have a way of going wrong.

"That is some good news," I said. "Now, if this scow would just finish docking."

About an hour later, we got our turn and Renaldo took us in with little trouble.

··**6**··

"**M**ickey," I said into the comm, "meet me at the lock."
"On my way," he said.

I usually take Mickey for two-person repossessions. He's got muscles if we need to undo any sabotage, and he's a pretty good mechanic if the ship has any emergency trouble.

"Renaldo, transmit the repossession order to station command. Get the docking fees paid. I want to be out of here in a half hour."

"Right," he said.

I stood up, got out from behind my desk and walked to the door.

"Take the seat, Alice. You have command."

"Captain," she said, and swooped around me to assume the chair.

I made my way to our equipment locker.

I grabbed a combat vest and my gun belt, then checked that the guns were loaded. I didn't expect trouble, but sometimes repos turned into shooting matches. I also pulled a comm earpiece from the locker and hooked it on my ear. I could get the implant, had thought about it several times, but decided I liked the removable ones well enough.

I also pulled out the repo case, a thin briefcase looking thing. I could open it up, pull out a set of wires, tap into the computer on the target vessel, send it the possession codes, and get the doors unlocked without having to try to hack the security systems. All vessels that were still bank collateral had to respond to these devices. Disabling bank access was generally subject to a kill order.

No one disabled the access.

I checked if there might be anything else I would need, and there were a number of tools I would take if I thought getting access would be difficult, but I expected the repo to go off without too much trouble, seeing as the delinquent was several star systems away.

I left the specialized gear in the locker and went to meet Micky at the air-lock.

"You ready?" I asked when I arrived.

"Yeah," he said. "Can't wait for my vacation."

I palmed the airlock control, the door shut behind us, and we waited for the pressure to equalize between us and the station. It took just a few seconds for the doors to open. The pressures were a near match.

I stepped out, Mickey following along behind me, and walked down the gangway. We went through the door at the bottom and found a pudgy little man who wore a black jacket with a New Corbi Customs logo emblazoned on the breast pocket.

He smiled, displaying perfectly straight, perfectly white teeth that seemed out of place above his paunch.

PARTED OUT

"Good afternoon, Gentlemen," he said. "I'm Anson Black, and I'm here to welcome you to New Corbi. Do you have your Federation ID chips on you?"

Some people had them embedded in their bodies. They get tired of carrying them around. I'm not one of those people. I know all the rationales regarding why you should embed the chip, including easier identification in the event of an early death, the ease of sliding through customs, the reduced risk of losing it, but I just couldn't let the Feds have that kind of hold on me. Maybe I have criminal tendencies, I don't know, but I don't like being tracked everywhere I go.

I reached into my pocket and pulled out the card with the embedded chip.

"How quaint," Anson said.

He waved his palm over it.

"Mr. Grimm. Glad to have you aboard. I hope your stay is pleasant.

Mickey held out his palm. He did not have the same issues with embedding it that I did.

"And Mr. Tucker. The same for you."

He turned back to me.

"Now, I received notice that you are here to repossess the Fleeting Star. We will, of course, assist you with anything you need in accordance with Federation Banking, Shipping, and Commerce regulations, but there are a couple minor issues that we will need to deal with before we can allow you access to the berth."

I glanced at Mickey while Mr. Official was spewing all that at me. I know it's his job, but it gets in the way.

When he mentioned *minor issues*, however, my attention went right back to him.

"What minor issues?"

"Well, the first is that the current owner has incurred quite significant docking fees that will have to be paid prior to our allowing it to leave its berth."

"We're prepared to pay those," I said. Part of the job. It made me wonder if they had ever dealt with a repossessed starship before.

"Good, that's good," he said.

"Is that it?" I asked.

"Oh, no. The other issue is that another captain submitted a salvage rights claim on the vessel."

"What? Who?" I asked in disbelief.

But I suspected I knew who. What I didn't know was how—how they could know about the ship, how they could even put in a claim on it, how the dock management would even let them touch the ship.

"Uh, I think his name was Captain Everly of the, uh..."

"Vulture," I said.

"No," said Anson said. "I think it's the Kestrel. You would think I would have better recall of these things."

He shrugged.

"No," I said. "Trust me, the ship is called The Vulture."

He tilted his head just a little and squinted, then shrugged again.

"If you say so. Now..."

I was running out of patience, but I had also recovered some of my equilibrium.

"No one can claim salvage on a ship that is still collateral in a loan. It's Federation regulation."

"On the contrary, they can if the property has been abandoned."

PARTED OUT

"Are you listening to this, Alice?" I asked. She had to be listening in via the comm. I always turned it on when I left the ship, and she always listened.

"Yes," she said through the earpiece, "and technically, he's right. However, the definition of abandoned is somewhat ambiguous."

"Three months idle is not abandoned."

"You are correct," said Anson. "Not usually, at least, but in this case, Captain Everly brought us a contract, signed between him and the owner of the Fleeting Star that clearly states the owner is abandoning the ship to Captain Everly and his salvage operation."

"That's not a valid contract. He can't sell the ship without the lender's approval."

"Yes, yes. We are aware of that, however, when we granted him access to the ship..."

"You've already granted them access to the ship! Why are we still here talking?"

I tried to push past him, to get to the ship, but he stepped in my way.

"Captain Grimm, please listen to me. When we granted him access, we were not aware that the original loan had not been paid. We requested authorization from the lender of record, and were informed that the debt had been paid and the owner of the ship was clear of all obligations."

"Didn't you think that stank, just a little?" I asked.

"It was not until your notice of intent to repossess," he said, furrowing his brow as if he had thought I was the one in the wrong, "and if you ask me, that came a little late—that we became aware the lender in the contract was a shell corporation, and that the contract was fraudulent."

"So it's my fault that you can't do proper diligence before allowing a salvage operation access to a ship?"

"No, no. It's just that, if you had transmitted your repossession order sooner, then none of this would have happened."

I wanted to put my hands to my head in frustration, squeeze the headache that was forming back into oblivion, but I couldn't afford to look like I was frustrated any more than I already had.

"Look," I said when I had myself under control, "you know we can't transmit those things before we dock. Delinquent owners sometimes have friends on station that will move a ship out before we can even get close to it."

Anson stood a little straighter, offended. "I hope you are not saying..."

"I'm sorry, I didn't mean to imply that happened here, or even would happen here. But it has happened in other places. Sometimes, they even try to destroy the ship before we can take it."

"That is..."

"Illegal, yes. But it happens. And if you don't do something to revoke Captain Everly's access to that ship, we will have to put in a call to the Federation. You could find yourself sued to the tune of a hundred billion credits, or more, by the bank, which I don't think your superiors would enjoy paying.

"And, just so you know, I'm certain that Captain Everly is dismantling that ship from the inside out and will have most of it moved into his ship before you even realize that he's going to leave the shell that remains in your dock, and he will never pay you the docking fees."

PARTED OUT

Right then, the worry I had hoped I would see on the smug man's face appeared.

"You wouldn't call in the Federation, would you?" he asked.

"If you don't get them off of that ship right this minute, I might have to. And if I don't, the bank will."

He turned away from me, took a few steps to put distance between us, and tapped a switch on his comm. He spoke hurriedly into it for a few moments, quiet enough that I could not hear, then he listened.

"I don't care how you do it," he said, losing his temper. "Get it done!"

After a few seconds composing himself, he turned back to us.

"They will be out of the ship in the next quarter hour," he said.

"With nothing removed."

"We will not allow them to take anything from the ship. I just need your commitment that you will not file any lawsuits against us."

It was obvious they didn't want the Feds involved, or that he personally didn't. It all stunk of some kind of scam, but it didn't bother me much what he was doing.

"Look, I just want the boat, and then we're out of here. I can guarantee you that my company, Grim Repossessions, will not file any sort of lawsuit against this station or its management as long as you get those vultures out of that ship and keep them from taking anything with them."

"Is that wise?" Alice asked into my comm. I ignored her. It wasn't wise to make that guarantee, but if I couldn't get the vultures out of that boat with the least damage possible, then we would be out any sort of fee until the lawsuits were finished, and I'd rather spend my time repossessing spacecraft than spend it attending court proceedings.

"Thank you," Anson said, looking a little less nervous.

"I cannot, however, guarantee that the bank will choose not to sue. I can keep our report to them simple, or I can explain all the details. Personally, if I can get the ship back to them in one piece, I think they will forgive the mishap. They probably wouldn't even need to know about it."

Anson tugged at his collar. I was glad to see it. I didn't want him comfortable.

"We have an understanding?" I asked.

"We do. They will be out, and they won't leave with anything they didn't go in with."

"Then lead us to the ship," I said. "I want to watch."

••7••

Mickey and I did our best to stay out of the way as station security took their places at the entrance to the Fleeting Star's birth. A dozen men, all dark uniformed and wearing riot helmets and combat vests staked themselves to either side of the gangway. Metal detectors and other equipment for ensuring that what belonged to the Fleeting Star remained with the Fleeting Stare were moved into place.

Our pudgy escort, Anson, had left us to ourselves and disappeared.

"I wish they'd hurry up," I said to Mickey. "The longer those vultures are in there, the more work we're going to have to do."

"We only have to get it up and running, right?"

"It has to pass inspection, too," I said. "If that Captain knows what's going on out here, he'll do his best to make it not pass."

"Why would he do that?"

"He'll want to make sure he has time to fight their eviction from the ship. He'll try to tie us up in court."

"He can't win, can he?"

"No, but he'll try. He paid the delinquent," I almost never use real names in public, "for the rights to that vessel. I'm sure that's where the delinquent's new cash reserves came from. He won't let it go without a fight. Since he'll know we're here to repossess the ship, he'll probably figure out that the delinquent hasn't got the funds to repay the fee, and he'll use everything he can to get as much of that ship into his holds as possible. It's the only way he'll not lose money on the deal."

The men were set in their places, their equipment ready. I expected that, at any moment, the order would be issued.

Anson chose that moment to return.

"Good news," he said as his short-legged steps carried him toward us. "I just finished reviewing the security video, and it does not appear that they have, as yet, removed anything from the ship."

"When will they be ordered out?"

"In just a minute, but first, I need your signature on these documents."

He offered a tablet to me, and on it, I could see a document covered with legalese.

"What's this?" I asked.

He lost a little of his confidence, and replaced it with a nervous twitch of his eyes.

"It is a document absolving us of any liability for any damage done to the Fleeting Star."

Despite his nervousness, he had balls, or his superiors did. I didn't even read it.

PARTED OUT

"I can't sign it," I said.

"You can't?" he asked.

"I don't have the authority to sign a document for my clients that commits them to an action they have not approved."

"But..."

"I already told you, I will not inform my client of this little misunderstanding if you get those bastards out of there before they can do too much damage. I won't sign anything, though, until I've seen the state of the ship after they are out. The quicker they are out, the less likely I'll have any reason to inform my client.

"It won't be me suing you. It will be them."

The hand holding the tablet out to me shook, then withdrew, taking the tablet with it.

"They just wanted your assurance..."

"No. They wanted to be legally absolved and protected from a lawsuit, and were hoping that I was new to this game. I've been doing it long enough to have taught others how to do it themselves. I don't sign anything before I know the condition of the ship, especially not when the document could be considered binding on my clients."

"You could comm them..."

There was something else going on, here. He was being far too insistent.

"Let me guess. You authorized their entry to the ship, and your superiors are holding you accountable."

His eyes darted toward the security people, then up toward the ceiling, glancing at the security cameras.

The he whispered. "You don't know what it's like. If you or your client sue the station, they will take it out of me," he said.

"Responsibility has its perks," I said. "I honestly don't care what trouble that would bring you, since you could so easily avoid it by ordering the Vulture's men out of the Fleeting Star right this minute. Why are you stalling?"

He looked up at the camera again, then back down at me.

He leaned in close to me this time, and whispered, even quieter, "This isn't the Kestrel's first trip to the ship."

He glanced up at the camera.

I looked at the ship.

Not the first time.

That meant there had been a previous trip, and while nothing may have left the ship yet, this time, at least some of the ship had already left.

What I couldn't believe is that Anson was letting it happen without Captain Everly paying the docking fees.

I turned away from the pudgy little man, looked out the expansive windows that let me see the hull of the ship I was supposed to repo, and spoke in a quiet voice into my comm.

"Did you get all that, Alice?" I asked

"I did," she said. "I'm contacting Elliot right now."

"I wonder," I said. "How many ships have they done this to?"

"I'll make sure I find out," she said.

I turned back to look at Anson.

"Get them out of that ship," I said, "or I can guarantee you that my clients will hear about this."

He looked at me, fear in his eyes. I don't know if it was his operation, or if his superiors frightened him that much, or maybe they didn't know about it, but at that moment, I didn't give a shit. I had to stop the destruction of that

PARTED OUT

ship, or I would have traveled out here for nothing, and been paid only my retainer for the second time in three months. My retainer was not nearly enough to cover all my costs, and those costs were mounting.

Anson turned away from me, spoke into his comm.

I turned to Mickey.

"I'm not getting my vacation, am I?" he asked.

"Not unless we get very lucky," I said.

Very lucky would mean that, on the first trip, Captain Everly took only what wasn't bolted down.

Anson disappeared as the first of Captain Everly's men exited the ship. Station security checked each of the men as they exited, took a few things, but it appeared that Everly's men generally complied with the order to leave everything where it was.

I waited, watching them, expecting to see Everly leave the ship with his crew, but he never came down the gangway. He must have sent his men to work without his supervision.

Of course, he had three times the crew I carry, just in the work detail, alone. He probably had another half dozen on board his ship. Salvage work required a lot more muscle than repo work.

When the stream of men petered out, I led Mickey over to the head security officer, a tall man, black mustache, long sideburns, and a hooked nose. He looked down on me, and even, to an extent, Mickey.

"What do you want?" he asked.

I waved my ident tag and showed him the tablet with our repossession order on it.

"I'd like access to the Fleeting Star. I need to find out how much damage has been done, and how much I'm going to have to fix before I can get it out of here."

He looked at my tablet, then spit on the floor at my boot.

"Repo men," he said. "You know what repo men, do? Legalized thievery."

"It's not thievery if someone hasn't paid their debt."

"Tell that to my brother," he said.

"He had something repossessed?" I asked.

"He had a ship once, tried to make a living with it. Spent his life savings on it. His wife got sick. He had to spend three months caring for her before she died. Then, just about the time he was going to go back out, your ilk came and took his ship, leaving him stranded with no wife, no ship, and no way to make any money. Ruined his life."

I watched him, waited for him to continue, but he was done. I could have argued that people don't normally lose their ships after three months of missed payments. The banks usually wait a lot longer than that. My guess is that his brother was in a heap of trouble long before his wife got sick.

But I wasn't going to tell him that.

"I'm sorry to hear that," I said. "I've never taken someone's property if they've only been delinquent for three months. Someone was far too aggressive, I think."

He blinked, I think surprised that I had agreed with him.

I didn't agree, but that wouldn't get my job done.

"Much too aggressive," he said. "They could at least have given him another chance, considering what he went through."

PARTED OUT

"I agree," I said. "Now, this boat here, he hasn't paid a single credit on it in a year, and he hasn't paid the docking fees, either, and those fees pay your salary, I'd bet."

I got a nod out of him. It was enough.

"If you let me in, I'll pay the docking fees and fly this thing out of here."

He smiled, and stood aside.

"I'll let you in," he said. "I don't think you'll be flying it out of here."

A knot formed in my stomach.

"Thank you," I said.

I wasn't going to ask him what he meant. I knew I'd find out on my own, soon enough.

I took the electronics out of my briefcase and plugged them into the socket next to the door.

The readout came up, and I quickly entered the codes I had been given by the bank.

They marked the ship as repossessed, relisted the ship under the ownership of the bank, and changed the lock sequence.

No one but me, my crew, or the bank, would now be able to enter the ship without permission. Even station security would be locked out.

I packed the electronics back into the case, palmed the lock open, and took my first step inside.

And, at first, I didn't see any real problems.

"It doesn't look too bad," Mickey said.

"It wouldn't," I said. "They'll have been working in one of two areas, the bridge, or the engine room."

"I'll check the engine room," Mickey said.

He didn't wait for my assent before turning to the aft and walking off.

The bridge was mine.

I headed forward. The bridge was located about a quarter of the way from the bow, on the top deck. We came in amidships in all ways that mattered.

It was a big ship, though most of it was cargo hold. A minimal crew of two could fly it from here to there while it was empty, but a complete operating crew numbered sixteen, most of them required for managing cargo and keeping the ship running from port to port.

I found the elevator and stepped in. I still hadn't seen any signs of the salvage operation. It was hard to believe so many of Everly's men had been inside this tub and there was so little evidence of it.

I stepped out of the elevator shaft at the top, hooked a right and followed the corridor to the bridge.

The door slid open.

Alice pinged my comm.

The scene before me was unmitigated disaster. Desks had been removed and stacked against the wall, cables were stripped out and rolled up, the command chair had been removed from its moorings and set in the middle of the room. All the screens had been taken down and set to one side.

An hour to remove, a week to put back together.

"Grimm," Alice said, pinging me again.

"What?" I asked, distracted.

I could feel the money draining from my account.

"I've got Captain Everly requesting to speak with you."

The trip through the ship's corridors had elevated my hopes, lulled me into thinking they hadn't damaged much.

PARTED OUT

I thumbed the camera on my comm and showed Alice what I was looking at. I panned it around the bridge of the Fleeting Star.

After she had seen the whole thing, she said, "So, now is not a good time. Should I tell him you'll get back to him?"

"Yes," I said. "I'll get back to him as soon as I rid myself of the urge to shoot him."

"Noted."

She clicked off.

I could only hope that Mickey had not found the same level of disrepair on his end of the ship that I had found on mine.

No. There was one other little ray of hope. At least, it looked like the equipment was all there and not permanently damaged.

Mickey pinged my comm.

"How's it look?" I asked.

"It could be worse," he said.

My hope turned sour.

"What does that mean?"

"I think all the parts are here. I won't be sure until I start putting the engines back together again."

I closed my eyes and imagined I was any other place but standing on the bridge of the Fleeting Star. I'd even let myself get blown up again.

··10··

I left Mickey to work on the Fleeting Star's engines and returned to the Grim Repo. I had some calls to make, but I was still seething, and I couldn't make the calls in that state. It wouldn't do to have my clients see me upset. They want to see a cool, calm, get the job done attitude, even when all the shit in the universe has just spewed forth to envelope you.

So I took a shower, long and hot, since we were hooked up to the station. The reclamation systems work great, but there's a limited amount of water when we're not docked, and it takes time to reclaim it. Stations, with their greater water reserves, make it easier to indulge.

When I finished my shower, I toweled off and pulled on a clean shirt before sitting down at the desk in my cabin.

I brought up the comm, found the bank's contact code and worked up a message.

"Hello Mr. Adams. We have just arrived on station and toured the Fleeting Star. Structurally, the Fleeting Star looks to be in good condition, and I would fly it out of here right now, if I could. Unfortunately, we've hit a couple snags that we are working to rectify. Apparently, the delinquent decided to remove a number of items from the Fleeting Star, many of which are required to be installed in order to pass inspection. It appears we stopped the removal in time, and that no parts are actually missing, but reinstalling them will delay our flight out by two or three days.

"I am terribly sorry for the delay."

I signed it with my usual, "Grimm," and sent it off. Since the message had to travel through a half dozen gates, plus through the space between us and the gates, I didn't expect to hear from them until about four hours later.

Then, I commed Alice.

My door opened.

"I'm right here," she said, and walked into the room.

I scrambled across the room to retrieve a pair of pants. Her golden eyes followed me the whole way.

"The least you could do is give me time to get completely dressed before you walk in," I said.

"Perhaps you shouldn't comm me until you're dressed," she said.

She had a point.

I pulled my pants on, buckled them, and returned to my desk.

I brought up the schematic of the Fleeting Star, then superimposed the images I took of the bridge's current state on top of it.

"They did some quick work," she said. "I can see already that one of the desks is missing completely."

PARTED OUT

"They didn't remove it from the ship, today. Maybe it's still aboard. Will it keep us from flying out of there?"

"No. You only need two desks for it to fly, and I see two plus the Captain's chair. More than enough.

"I'll need your help getting those things reinstalled," I said.

"Agreed," she said. "You'll probably have to hire a crew to help get it done, too."

"A crew?" I had already thought of the possibility, but I had hoped to avoid it. A crew would eat into our profits.

"Yes, a half dozen if you want out of here in the next couple days. We're qualified for repair work, but this is installation, recalibration, re-certification."

I slammed my hand against the wall. It hurt, made a loud slapping noise, but I wasn't stupid enough to punch with a fist.

"Tell me what else," Alice said.

I superimposed the engine room on the schematic for her.

"I see. You wanted me to tell you that the bridge would be a simple job."

"Yes," I said. It hadn't looked simple to me, but I had hoped she would tell me different.

"The engine room is simpler. He'll need some muscle, though."

"Yes, I know. Hire three," I said, cringing as I said it, "to go along with the six for the bridge. Get them working today."

"I'll do what can be done," she said. "Now, about Captain Everly. Are you going to talk to him? He's been hitting the comm every ten minutes since you returned."

"Persistent," I said.

"Very."

"Fine, I'll take it the next time he comms."

Alice leaned over my desk and tapped the comm active. "He's on the comm right now," she said.

I could see his face. He didn't look happy. But then, he'd paid William Baty a pretty considerable sum for the privilege of ripping apart the Fleeting Star and selling the parts. I could understand why he'd be upset.

Alice hadn't turned on the transmission, so Captain Everly was still not aware I was watching.

I turned to Alice. "Do you keep these things from me on purpose? Do you enjoy it?"

"Grimm," she said. "You know I don't have the capacity to *enjoy* things. It is purely an exercise in ordering priorities, and my impression was that Captain Everly was your lowest priority. Was I wrong?"

"No. Get on hiring those contractors."

She turned and left me to deal with Captain Everly.

I turned back to the screen displaying Everly's hooked nose and activated the transmission.

"Captain," I said.

"It's about time," he said. "What the hell do you think you are doing, convincing station security to kick my men off my ship."

"Your ship? You are, unfortunately, mistaken. William Baty took you for a ride. The Fleeting Star belongs to Antarra First Intergalactic Bank."

"You're lying. You're just trying to steal it out from under me," he said. "I've already got my lawyer working on a lawsuit against you and your company."

A bluff, or stupidity. I was betting on bluff.

"No you don't," I said. "You had to notice, when you first entered the Fleeting Star, that its lender access codes were still active. Isn't that the first thing you people do? Check the registration, the LACs? If you had contacted your lawyer, he would have told you about the pile of shit you stepped into, and would have advised you to walk away."

"I don't walk away from anything," he said, his eyes flashing.

"You should walk away from this one," I said. "I'll show you."

I brought up the documents he would need to verify my claims; title with the bank listed as owner, registration, a statement showing an amount still owed that far exceeded Captain Everly's payment to William Baty.

When they were sent, Captain Everly glanced down at them and frowned. He spent just about three seconds looking them over.

"Fakes," he said. "William showed me the real documents. The statement showed he owed far less. What I paid him covered the difference. The ship is mine."

"Did you try to register it?"

"You don't need to register a ship that you're going to salvage for parts."

Which was true.

"If you had tried to register it, you would have learned right then that Mr. Baty had swindled you. He took you for a ride, and you paid for the privilege. The documents are not fakes, Captain Everly. Do your due diligence. Comm the bank. Complain all you want, but I proved sufficiently to station security, and I'll have no problem proving it to the courts."

"You're an asshole," said Captain Everly.

"Perhaps," I said. "At least I'm not a toilet."

"You'll regret making an enemy of me," he said.

Captain Everly's hand came up, slammed down on his comm, and disconnected.

"I doubt it," I said to the now blank comm.

I might regret a lot of things, but I don't think I'll ever regret making him an enemy. I had dozens of enemies already. What was one more?

••11••

I got up from my desk, dashed out into the corridor, and ran to the bridge. I didn't think I had much time.

I burst onto the bridge, startling Eddy and Renaldo. Even Alice turned to see who had barged in before returning to her work.

"Captain," Eddy said. "Is something wrong?"

"Not wrong, not exactly."

I turned to Alice.

"Do you have workers hired, yet?" I asked.

"Still working on it," she said without looking up from her desk. "The hiring requirements aboard this station are tedious to navigate, and you've only given me ten minutes to do it."

"Get it done while you and Renaldo make your way to the Fleeting Star. I want you overseeing the repairs, and Renaldo needs to load up with weapons for both him and Mickey."

That got their attention.

"Weapons, Captain?" Renaldo asked.

"A precaution. My negotiations with Captain Everly did not go as well as he hoped, and he seems to have taken a disliking to me. I don't want to believe that he would take it to another level, but..."

Renaldo stood.

"On it."

"Hurry," I said. "Mickey's over there alone."

Alice looked up from her desk.

"But the lock on the Fleeting Star..."

"Has been compromised once," I said. "Who knows if Captain Vulture over there has friends on this station. I hope not, and considering the way things went with station management, I don't think he has friends high up on the chain. But a dozen extra thugs could make short work of us."

Alice's eyes narrowed as she stared at me.

"You said something to him, didn't you? You said something to stir him up. You couldn't just send him off without insulting him."

"I tried," I said. I did, too.

"But you couldn't resist, could you?"

"He insulted me first."

She stood up, toggled her desk off.

"Your inability to control your anger makes more trouble for us," she said.

I could almost think she was angry, despite that not being possible.

"In this instance," I said, "it wasn't anger that spurred my tongue."

"Then what was it?"

"I was waiting for the opportunity, and he gave it to me."

"I'll never understand," she said, then walked past me and left the bridge.

Renaldo followed her out.

Eddy looked at me and smiled.

"So it's just you and me," she said, shaking her head just enough as an enticement, but not so much that it was obvious.

"It is," I said.

I sat down at my desk, brought up the stations I would need. Eddy had been on duty for at least twelve hours. She needed a rest.

"Why aren't you going over there?" she asked.

"You need a rest, I'm waiting for a response from the bank, and I've got a project I need to work on."

"Still researching those weapons?" she asked.

I looked up, betraying my surprise that she knew.

"What are you talking about?" I asked. I knew it was a poor attempt to hide my surprise, but it was all I could think of.

"I know you're still researching who made those weapons we stumbled across a couple months ago. You filled a whole memory cell with information on them."

"I did?"

She smiled. It was a pleasant, pleased with herself smile, not a devious conniving smile. I had never thought of her as devious, before.

"I watch you," she said, then looked down a little, "I see things."

"Like?"

"Like the memory cell you took from the computer supply room. I saw it attached to your desk in your cabin a couple weeks ago. I watch the data streams to and from the ship, too, and I noticed that you've sent a lot of traffic through Elliot, and it's all been encrypted. You never used to encrypt your traffic to Elliot."

I wonder what other clues I've given off.

"Anything else?" I asked.

"Just that you're hiding in your cabin more than usual," she said.

"From that, you guessed I was researching those weapons?"

"Yes, Grimm," she said, her voice soft and vulnerable as she said it.

Grimm. She said my name on the bridge, a mistake she hadn't made in two years.

But it wasn't a mistake. She'd done it on purpose. She saw we were alone and took the opportunity. It made me feel good. Even after two years of suffering my rejections, she still wanted me.

She looked so hopeful, sitting in her chair, her hands clasped in front of her, her brown hair pulled back to expose the creamy texture of her skin. She presented a problem I had yet to deal with since she came aboard, and if she was daring to use my name on the bridge, despite the rules, I knew it was getting close to the time when I'd have to deal with it, one way or another.

Only, I liked her, and she was a good crew member. I trusted her, perhaps not the same way that I trusted Alice, but I relied on her. I couldn't just let her go.

And if this were any other problem that I couldn't solve on this ship, I'd talk to Alice, but Alice would not even know where to start in solving this problem.

PARTED OUT

"We're still on the bridge, Eddy," I said.

"I know, but there's no one else here, and I thought..."

"Not on the bridge."

Her smile turned down just a little.

"Yes, Captain."

"Now, tell me, what makes you think that secrecy, a borrowed memory cell, and encrypted communications to Elliot means I'm researching those weapons?"

"Because that's what I'd do," she said.

It made sense. Her specialty—ship's weapons. All of my activity started right after we finished that job. If she noticed it early enough, she'd have to connect it.

Connect it, use it. Had she done some research on her own? Had she compromised us? I hesitated to ask because I didn't want to find out. If she had, our backups were at risk—our backups with all of my own research. I couldn't ask Eddy about it, either, because I didn't want to confirm it for her. Right now, she was only speculating. Right now, if the Feds showed up at our door because of her, it might look like professional curiosity.

But I didn't even know if she was doing her own research. I was just speculating.

Damn you, Mira, why did you have to make me so suspicious of every woman alive?

And right then, I knew I had to message Mira, see what she had to say about my situation with Eddy. Mira had used me for her own ends, and I didn't trust her with a single credit, anymore, but that didn't keep me from wishing she were on the Grim Repo right then. It didn't keep me from wanting to share a bed with her again.

::53::

I couldn't tell her about our research, not with her being a Fed—that was a surprise—but the other part, the relationship part, it would be good to hear her voice, her opinion.

The comm beeped. It was the collections agent from Antarra First.

"I've gotta take this, Eddy. Go get a nap. I'll wake you in six."

"Captain," she said, clearly disappointed at being dismissed.

But she needed the rest, and I needed some space to think.

When the door slid shut behind her, I started the message playing.

I had to listen to it three times before I could give up my thoughts of Eddy and Mira to focus on what it said.

·· 12 ··

I took Antarra First Galactic contracts because they paid well. If I took contracts based on who was easy to work with, they would be last on my list. They always wanted everything done now, and they didn't generally seem to understand that sometimes, circumstances are outside of our control.

So when I finally managed to comprehend the text of their agent's message, I marked it for a slow death and closed the comm.

"What the hell do they want me to do? I can't fly a ship that doesn't have engines or control desks."

There was no one on the bridge to hear my complaints.

A moment later, I opened the comm, returned the message to the land of the living. I would need to have it for future reference.

MARK FASSETT

Attn: Mr. Grimm, Grim Repossessions

We received your message, and a two day delay is acceptable, considering the circumstances. However, penalties will apply for a delivery that exceeds your original target date by more than that amount.

Aneis Uwe
Recovery Agent
Antarra First Galactic Bank

I wasn't surprised, as much as frustrated. Two days. I was only estimating, guessing, and they took it as carved in stone.

I commed Alice.

She picked up after a few moments.

"Grimm?" she asked as she connected.

"How's the hiring going?"

"I've just contacted a couple outfits. Looking for a few to price against them."

"Get 'em in there," I said. "Do what you can to find the best, and get 'em in. We have two days."

"Two days?" she asked.

"Got a message back from the bank. That's all they're going to give us before they start penalizing us."

"I'll get it done," she said, and hung up.

That's why I like Alice. She doesn't complain, except about me.

I sat for a moment, the silence of the bridge a nice interlude from the activity and the stress of the day. I switched the screens so they showed the view off our

::56::

stern, which gave me a partial look at the stars outside the station. A gantry blocked some of it, but it was better than the forward view, which showed nothing but millions of tons of girders, hoses, and piles of equipment used in the maintenance of the ships in dock.

I let my thoughts drift in that moment, trying to think of nothing, hoping a solution to getting that ship out of dock and back to the bank would pop into my head—something other than throwing my money at it.

Because that's what additional workers were; my money.

Banks pay in two ways for repossessions. One way, they provide a cut of the expected sale price of the ship after I return it to them, plus reimbursements for certain expenses, such as any repairs necessary to get the ship flying again.

The other way, I get a good sized retainer, and then a lower cut of the resale price, but I pay for incidental expenses out of my cut. This keeps me flying in the case of disasters, but when disasters strike, they wipe out profits unless I can keep the costs to a minimum.

And the restoration of the Fleeting Star to something resembling operational would eat huge portions of my profit. The penalties for being late, even more of it.

I ran some calculations through my desk, hoping to find an optimal solution. I couldn't find one that didn't cut my profit in half.

It was all the fault of that Captain Everly and his demolition crew over there on the Vulture.

With no one on the bridge, I slammed my hand against my desk and let loose, cursing William Baty, Captain Everly, and his whole crew in every way I could imagine. Then I screamed at the top of my lungs, the sound of it echoing back to me from every metallic surface.

"Grimm? Are you okay?" Alice asked through the comm after my scream ended.

I looked down, saw her face. Slamming the desk with my fist had activated it.

"I'm fine," I said. "We're going to lose half our profit, no matter what we do, but I'm fine."

I wasn't. She knew it. She stared into her comm, examining me, probably waiting for another outburst.

"I've got a list of bids to send you, if you want to see them."

I didn't.

"Send them."

"I'll mark the two I think will do the best job," she said.

"I want the two that will do the quickest job," I said.

"They're the same as the best," she said.

"Of course. I'm just pissed that we have to pay anyone. If that pompous little customs official hadn't let Captain Everly aboard the Fleeting Star, we'd be out of here."

The list of contractors came up on my screen.

I looked it over. I didn't really need to, though. Alice had marked the ones I would have picked.

"Grimm," Alice said. "What if..."

"Stop, Alice. I know what you're going to say. That pompous little prick is going to be getting a visit from me. I may not be able to sue him, but I might be able to convince him to pay our expenses."

She stared into the comm for a moment, so still that I thought maybe the signal had been interrupted, until I heard a noise in the background and she turned to look.

And then I realized I had surprised her.

PARTED OUT

When she turned back to the comm, she said, "Captain, for once, you *were* thinking what I was thinking."

I smiled. She didn't, her face remaining as emotionless as ever.

"One of these days, Alice, you'll learn how to smile."

"I doubt it," she said.

"In the meantime, hire the contractors you chose. Get them in there, get them working. If I can't save money on this end, I don't want to lose on the other."

And if I could just find that little man and intimidate him some more, I might not have to lose anything at all.

··13··

With Eddy sleeping, I had to stay on the ship. I could run most of the things I needed to do while we were in dock from any desk in the ship, but I couldn't run them remotely from my portable comm. The portable comms could do a lot of things, but that wasn't one of them. If it were at all safe to allow access to critical systems aboard the ship from a portable comm, I'd do it. But no captain in his right mind would do that sort of thing. You don't want your weapons hacked in the middle of a firefight, or your navigation systems, either, for that matter.

You can't keep them from trying. You still have to be able to communicate with other ships and the dock, even your own people throughout the ship, but communications runs on a separate system with its own storage that is copied to the primary system storage only after a series of data scrubbing that removes any potential hack attempts. Our core system doesn't access that storage, except when we specifically tell it to, or when we back up that storage.

Having the two systems separated frustrated me at that moment, because it kept me aboard instead of trudging off in search of Anson Black, but I wasn't about to change it—not after having pissed off Captain Everly. I was certain he was aboard his ship right then, trying to hack into our systems. It's what I would have done. Hell. I had done it.

I passed the time waiting for Eddy to wake by heading to the gym and lifting weights. I'd give anything for free weights, but aboard the ship, free weights are more trouble than they're worth. So I was stuck using the resistance machine, which works, but is not ideal. I'd buy a new one—there are new ones that are supposed to do a much better job of mimicking free weights—but I don't want to spend the time or the money installing them.

After I got through my routine, I took a quick shower, grabbed a roast beef sandwich—not actual beef from a cow, but something that resembled it—to eat and took it back to the bridge.

I could comm Anson Black, but I thought personal attention would do a better job of bringing about the results I wanted.

I checked the clock.

Another four hours until Eddy was due back.

As I sat on the bridge, chewing my sandwich, I contemplated comming Alice again, but knew she would just look at me with those golden eyes of hers and suggest that the interruption was wasting time. She'd comm me if she needed anything.

I also contemplated working up a message for Mira, asking her if she could look into this William Baty and see if he was up to no good, but decided that her Fed sensibilities might work against me. The other problem with that idea was that merely thinking of her swirled my thoughts. Knowing that she hadn't really hated my guts, that her attempt to steal my ship wasn't motivated by a personal desire to double-cross me, and that she might actually even love me, but that her job got in the way— knowing all that made it hard to not chase her down and try to find out if there was anything there. But my desire to avoid the Feds kept me from following up with her—that, and the withering golden-eyed glare that I would receive from Alice if she ever found out.

My thoughts turned to my research on those weapons, and I contemplated doing more, but quickly remembered that my research was stuck in the backups at the moment, unreachable.

Which left me with little to do except sit and stare at the monitors while my money drained out through the giant hole the Vulture and William Baty had opened in my wallet.

And then, I realized I didn't have nothing to do.

I brought up my comm, brought up everything I could find on the Vulture that I could glean out of the New Corbi station's docking registry. It wasn't a lot, but it was more than I expected.

Most of it was even semi-legally obtained. Being a certified repossession specialist, I can legally access recent docking data of any of the ships I am chasing. You have to enter the ident of the ship, as well as your own ident, which will inform anyone who looks that I'm chasing them, but the data is useful, and most delinquents don't even think to check the registry to see if anyone is on to them. Of course, the information costs credits, and a lot of them don't have the credits to check, which is why they're not making their required payments on their ships.

One of the dodgy things about the registry is that, if I have the ident of a ship, I can look it up, even if I don't have a contract to chase it down. I pay the fee, put in the ident, call it good. And since Captain Everly and I had contact out by the jump gate, I had his ident.

And while it's not legal for me to look into a ship that I don't have a contract to retrieve, the penalty is a small fine. The only way I'll have to pay the penalty is if Captain Everly looks into the registry, sees my query about his ship, and reports it. I was more than happy to pay any future fines.

So I paid the fee.

Captain Everly had visited the station on nearly a hundred occasions. The ship was not registered there, it wasn't even registered in any systems nearby, but it seemed to be making pretty regularly scheduled stops.

Interestingly enough, his contact each time was Anson Black. Every time. It wouldn't be terribly surprising if New Corbi were a small outpost and had only a few employees on station at any one time, but they weren't small. They were decidedly mid-sized, with the security force to prove it. I would have thought that once, at least once, Anson would have been off duty when Captain Everly paid the station a visit.

It made me suspicious, especially with Anson's obvious desire to keep the Feds out of the place, and out of this situation.

Maybe it wasn't William Baty that was the problem here, at all.

:: 64 ::

PARTED OUT

I cut myself off from the station feed. I couldn't have what I was about to send out go through any channels that Anson or Captain Everly could tap.

I looked at the clock on my desk, its time slowly ticking up toward the next duty change.

Three hours left. I'd spent an hour looking through the data.

I coded a message to Elliot, the man who could find anything, and usually did. I asked him to look into Anson Black and Captain Everly and see what connections he could find.

I wouldn't hear back from him before Eddy came back, and might not hear back from him before I could track Anson down, but I'd certainly hear back from him before we had to leave with the Fleeting Star. And even if I couldn't use whatever Elliot found against Anson and Everly myself, I might be able to use it for leverage with the bank.

As far as I was concerned, the only potential downside was angering station management and being denied docking rights there in the future, but if I couldn't make a profit because of them, because of Anson, I didn't really care. I hadn't been to New Corbi before, and I had done all right.

But I was betting that whatever was going on was a scheme cooked up by Anson and Everly.

I just had to figure out what it was, and then figure out how I could use it.

··14··

Eddy relieved me from my duty on the bridge, her eyes quite a bit brighter than when she left.

"I'm going to go check on the Fleeting Star," I said. "Lock all the hatches and don't let anyone in while I'm gone."

"You want me to come with you?" she asked, her voice full of hope. She didn't want to be left alone.

"No," I said. "I sent a query to Elliot, and I'm waiting for a response. I want to be notified as soon as it comes in."

"You could just forward it to your comm," she said.

"I don't want it going through the station," I said.

"Something up?" she asked.

"Maybe. Just comm me and ask me to come back to the ship. Don't say Elliot's name."

She nodded by dipping her head a little between her shoulders. Her hair fell forward to obscure her face. It made me wish my desires were different, made me wish I understood why I was reluctant to accept her advances. I'd never been reluctant with anyone, ever, before.

I turned to leave, anxious to be on my way, and unwilling to follow that line of thought any further.

But before I left, I looked back at her.

"Make sure you lock the hatches," I said.

She looked up at me.

"I will," she said. "And Captain?"

"Yes," I said.

"I'm... I'm sorry, about before," she said.

"Don't worry about it," I said.

I waited for a moment, as she looked like she had something else to say, but when no other words were forthcoming, I left.

I went straight to the equipment locker, put on my armored vest, strapped on my weapons, my comm.

As I did so, I couldn't get Eddy's face out of my mind, the way she looked when she said she was sorry. So contrite, so willing.

I went to the airlock, waited for it to open.

I'd slept with almost every female that ever worked aboard my ship. Every single one of them was competent to do their job. I don't hire people who aren't capable, but I had hired women like Eddy and Mira as much for their interest in me as their looks and my desire. I don't pretend to be anything other than what I am. My business isn't easy, I'm never home for dinner, or ever. So I took what pleasure I could when I could find it.

I stepped into the airlock, let it shut behind me.

If Alice weren't a sim, if she had any feelings at all, I'd probably find her attractive, too.

If Mira hadn't done what she'd done, if she hadn't had a purpose for signing on...

PARTED OUT

Maybe that was why, after Mira, I hadn't slept with anyone. Perhaps I feared losing myself to another woman that would be as false with me as Mira had been.

The airlock door between me and the gangway opened, and I stepped out, waited until the airlock shut behind me, then set the hard-lock code.

Maybe that was all that was. Two years of wishing I could follow my primal desires and sleep with Eddy, when I knew that was what she wanted. Two years of denying myself because I was afraid.

I walked down the gangway.

I knew what I had to do.

"When this is over," I said to myself, "I'm going to sit down and talk with Eddy."

A hand came to rest on my shoulder.

"If you think this is over," said a rough voice that I didn't recognize, "then you're going to be disappointed."

I turned and found myself confronting a man almost as large as Mickey, with far more hair, a huge tattoo down the side of his face, and a beard that reached the middle of his chest.

We were out of the Grim's camera range. It wouldn't surprise me if the station cameras were off, too.

I reached for my gun.

"I wouldn't do that," said another voice.

A chilling circle of gun barrel pressed against my neck.

"What do you want?" I asked, fearing I knew the answer. I'd been so caught up in my thoughts about Eddy and Mira that I hadn't been paying attention to my surroundings.

"Captain Everly wants to see you," said tattoo man.

I tried to turn and catch a glimpse of the man who had the gun to my neck, but caught sight of two other men standing by. They looked nearly as grungy as tattoo man, and I would have bet my ship they also worked for Everly.

"You going to come nice? Or do we have to carry you."

One of the other men, a lanky sort that smelled like he hadn't showered in days, came up behind me and relieved me of my weapons.

"It looks like I have a date with your Captain," I said.

The man with the gun pushed it into my neck.

"Get walking."

I started walking, directed by a gun and the muscled arms of tattoo man. I hadn't even had a chance to access my comm. Eddy and Alice wouldn't know where I was, and unless Alice called Eddy to ask for help with something—a highly unlikely event—it could be a long time before they figured out I'd gone missing, each one thinking I was with the other.

··15··

I had hoped to see security come to my rescue during the fifteen minute trip to the Vulture's berth, but I didn't catch sight of a single uniformed officer. Even the other spacers on the concourse ignored our little procession, going so far as to move out of the way. The gun had moved from my neck to a more concealed spot with the barrel ramming into my side through a gap in my armored vest, or I would have shouted out for help and taken my chances.

Maybe I should have shouted out, anyway. Alice could have reconstructed me, probably, but after the first bullet, there was no guarantee the second wouldn't end up in my brain.

I had little desire to take that chance. And with the way the other spacers wouldn't even make eye contact, I suspected they wouldn't take that chance, either.

Everly's men took me up a gangway and into an airlock that looked like it hadn't seen a good scrub-down in an eon, with streaks of dirt and grease on almost every surface.

When the airlock cycled, the interior of the Vulture looked hardly any different than the airlock. The ship was used hard, and used a lot. I didn't have any doubt that it would never see another owner. It wouldn't have surprised me to find that Captain Everly bought a ship, used it up, salvaged it, and then bought another.

I tried to project calm, like I didn't care they could put an end to me. Captain Everly may have been angry with me, pissed even, but I didn't think he would murder me. Not yet. It would be a lot harder to get what he wanted out of a dead man.

But I've been wrong before. Whatever I tried to project, I was anything but calm inside.

The corridor led forward along the spine of the ship. We passed several doors and a couple muscled men—my guess was that they were useful in pulling dead ships apart—before they stopped me outside a closed door.

The leader of the little gang palmed the door open, and thrust me into the room.

It wasn't opulent, but it wasn't a grease pit like the rest of the ship seemed to be. It had a long table at the center, surrounded by a dozen chairs. The far wall had a screen embedded in it. A podium stood in the corner.

A lone man sat at the table, his crooked nose making it painfully clear who it was. He looked a little different than I remembered from the comm, even thinner than I had thought, a scrawny skeleton of a man, but with strength in his features, nonetheless. He had his hands clasped on the table in front of him.

He didn't stand to greet me.

"Sit," Captain Everly said.

PARTED OUT

I took one of the chairs. The cushion was still in good shape. It gave me the impression Captain Everly did not use the room often.

"Why am I here?" I asked.

I knew why. He wanted some sort of payment to cover his losses, but I wanted to hear him say it.

"You have to ask?"

"I do," I said. "I thought we had cleared the air during our last conversation."

A finger on Everly's hand twitched, but his eyes remained locked on mine.

"You raised some issues. I've looked into them. You may be in the right, but you're where I live."

He tapped a spot on the table, and a desk woke up in front of me. It had a document open.

"What's this?" I asked.

"It's a contract," he said. "Read it."

"You tell me what it says." I wasn't going to bother to read it. Any contract he shoved in front of me was for his benefit, only.

"I'll give you the overview. It states that you and I are in business together on the Fleeting Star, and as the one who found the ship first, I get sixty percent of the profit. In exchange, I'll ensure that you can get that boat out of this station."

I resisted the urge to laugh in his face. I didn't need his help.

"I'm not signing it," I said.

His pinky twitched this time. He was making every effort, it seemed, to remain calm.

"I would think through that decision again," he said.

"Why? I'm not going to give sixty percent of my profits to you. I'm not going to give you a single credit. It's not my fault you paid for rights that don't exist to a man that had no business selling those rights in the first place.

"It doesn't seem that we have much else to talk about. Would you mind if I leave, now? I've got business to attend to."

"You can go," he said.

I stood up, went to the door.

"Captain Grimm," said Everly.

I stopped at the door, but didn't look at him.

"I'll give you twenty-four hours to think it over. And I do suggest you think hard. There are difficulties, sometimes, getting a ship off this station."

There was the threat I had expected.

"I've noticed that," I said, then stepped up to the door.

I had to palm the door open myself.

My two captors followed me down the corridor, all the way to the airlock.

At least it hadn't turned violent, as I had expected. He wasn't quite the man I expected. A business man, shady, but not a pirate. Not quite.

I didn't start shaking until I was back on the main concourse.

··16··

The clamor aboard the Fleeting Star's bridge made it far too difficult to talk there.

I found Alice amidst that clamor, pulled her into an adjoining compartment filled with electronic gear, and shut the door. Buried behind the gear, I noticed a beverage dispenser. The compartment must have been a small kitchen, at some point, before the delinquent loaded it with junk.

"What's got you spooked?" she asked as soon as the door shut.

"How did you know?"

"Your pupils are dilated, your breathing is a bit erratic, and your body is shaking."

"You can see all that?" I asked.

"Yes. Most of the time, you've just been in a firefight, but this is different. You don't have your weapons on you."

I didn't, either. I wasn't about to ask for them back as I left. I didn't see them in plain sight, and I wasn't going to wait while they found them. I had wanted off that ship.

"I had a personal chat with Captain Everly."

"Personal?"

"His thugs grabbed me as I left the Grim, took my weapons, then dragged me over to that vulture's ship where he presented me with a contract that gave him sixty percent of our earnings on this trip."

"You didn't sign it," she said.

"No."

"And he let you leave," she said.

"He said he's giving me twenty-four hours to think about it. Any chance we can get this tub flying in less than twenty-four?"

She shook her head. "Not a chance. Thirty-six is the best I can do."

"Thirty-six. That's not making me happy."

"It's the earliest we can get the inspector in here."

"You've got to be kidding," I said. "He can't have a whole lot to do on this station. Any way we can bribe him to get him here earlier?"

"No," she said. "He's planet-side, on vacation."

I wanted to turn and punch the electronics, but I couldn't allow myself the pleasure. I needed the boat to fly, not another repair bill.

"All right," I said. "Then I need you to come up with all of the scenarios you can think of that Captain Everly might try to keep this boat stuck here. Bribes, sabotage, anything at all. We need to be ready for whatever he might try."

"Anticipating what irrational people might do is not my strength," she said.

"I know. But do it anyway. You don't necessarily have to think like him, just think of all the scenarios that could keep the boat from flying."

PARTED OUT

"You should message Mira," she said.

I blinked. My mouth probably fell open, too.

"That's the last thing I expected to hear you say."

"She's a Fed, Grimm. Everly is threatening us. We have every legal right to take this ship."

"Mira can't get here in time," I said. I hoped. Even the mention of her name caused me to think about her, her and Eddy and what I had been thinking about when Everly's men accosted me. They were a distraction right now, one that I didn't need.

"Mira can't, but there should be a Federation cruiser close enough that could get Everly out of our hair."

I shook my head.

"No," I said. "I'll think about it, but any Fed cruiser that came around would want us to stay and provide a statement, at the least. We can't afford to stay. The repair costs are going to eat half of our profits, and any delay getting this wreck back to the bank will eat the other half in penalties."

"I'm aware," she said. "But if we don't get the ship out of here at all, you'll be out the repair cost, and not get any of the resale price to cover the repair cost."

She had a point.

But it reminded me of one of the reasons I had left the Grim in the first place.

"I have a plan to get the repair cost covered," I said.

"What is it?"

"I think Anson Black and Captain Everly have a deal. Maybe Anson works for Everly, maybe he just takes bribes, maybe he's running the whole thing and he has deals with other salvagers, too, but I think they search out ships in financial distress, get the owners to sell for a low-ball offer, and split the salvage income."

"Banks would have found out about it," Alice said.

"Not if they forged records of ship departures. Anson was very worried that I might bring the bank in on this—the bank or the Feds."

Then she made the insight.

"You're going to blackmail him into paying for the repair crews," she said.

"Right, and then we fly the ship back to the bank, on time, and keep the entire profit we would have if Anson and Everly hadn't gotten in the way in the first place."

"It sounds like a way to get yourself killed," she said.

"Anson won't kill me," I said. I hoped. "He doesn't have those kinds of balls. Besides, it's in his best interest to get me out of his hair with a minimum of fuss."

"Either that," she said, "or decide he doesn't trust you to keep your word and kill you, despite the fuss."

"I thought you said you couldn't anticipate what irrational people do," I said.

"I can't. If Anson chooses to kill you, it's an entirely rational choice."

··17··

I poked my head into the engine room. Around the cluster of engines that were still not all back in place, tool trays and parts described a haphazard style of working. The six men we had hired leaned against any upright surface, talking, drinking coffee (or whatever passed for coffee on New Corbi).

I found Mickey with his head deep inside the innards of an engine and lost my temper.

"Mickey!"

My shout echoed across the engine room.

He pulled himself out.

"What's up, Grimm?"

I waved my arms about at the men who were standing around. They all looked alert, now, and wary, standing a little straighter, not leaning.

"I'm not paying these guys to stand around. When I hire people to work for us, *you* stand around and supervise, not the other way around."

"They ain't standin' around," he said. "They're on break."

"Break?"

"Yeah," he said, running a grease-streaked hand through his hair. "Fifteen minutes every two hours. It's in their contract."

Which I hadn't read. Alice had. It would have been nice of her to tell me the details.

"Then what are you doing with your head in there?" I asked, somewhat irrationally.

"I get my break after we're done," he said. "The sooner we're done, the sooner I get a week of ale and women."

My bet would be more ale than women, but I wasn't going to place bets.

"How long until it's finished?" I asked.

"Eighteen hours, I think. Then they've gotta be tested and all," Mickey said.

Eighteen hours. We had twenty four. Twenty three, perhaps.

"Not fast enough. Do what you can to get it done in sixteen. I'll get the inspector in here to start the certification process early, if I can."

"You think they'll do that?"

"No idea."

I glanced over at the men standing around. Engine jocks if I'd ever seen any. They all looked like Mickey, except for one scrawny looking guy that couldn't have been more than five and a half feet tall.

Fifteen minute breaks every two hours. If they gave up those breaks, it would give us the two hours I wanted.

"Hey," I said to them, "Who runs your crew?"

"I do," said the scrawny guy.

PARTED OUT

"What would it take to get you to give up your breaks on this job?"

He laughed. "Give up our breaks? Man, your crazy. They're in the contract. Besides, we need the breaks. Doin' this work ain't no simple job you can do without some rest."

"What would it take?"

"Time and a half," the guy said. "For the whole job."

Fifty percent more was not the answer I had been hoping to hear. Not when I really didn't want to pay them anything at all.

"Ten percent bonus," I said.

He laughed derisively.

"No way, man. Not worth it. I'd get fined if I made these monkeys work without their legally mandated breaks."

I turned away from him and triggered my comm.

"Alice?"

"Grimm?"

"How are we paying these guys down here?" I asked.

"Lump sum for the job."

"And the fifteen minute breaks?"

"Legally required on New Corbi," she said. "No flexibility without the risk of huge fines for the company."

"What's the amount of the lump sum?"

"One hundred ten thousand," she said.

"Robbery," I said.

"They're supposed to be the best."

"All right, thanks."

"Why are you asking?"

"I want to see if I can get these engines ready a few hours earlier. I want to be able to, in a pinch, fly this thing out without the certifications."

MARK FASSETT

"Grimm, you can't do that," she said.

"I'm not saying we're going to. I just want to have options. Right now, we don't have options."

"If you fly it without certification, you won't have any idea whether these guys did their work well, or not."

"Mickey's watching them down here, you're watching them up there. If I can't trust you two to make sure shit goes back together correctly, who can I trust?"

"So you're saying you want the bridge to be ready to go, too."

"Do your best," I said. "Make sure at least one console is working before Everly's timer expires."

She clicked off.

I turned back to the scrawny guy, but made sure to take in his fellows, too.

"How about this," I said. "You take your breaks, I don't care. But get this job done in sixteen hours, and I'll give you a ten percent bonus."

"Ten percent? That's it?"

"I won't pay it to your company," I said. "I know they're making fifty percent over the cost of your labor. Every company does that. I'll put that ten percent bonus, eleven thousand credits split between the six of you, straight into your pockets."

Their eyes went wide.

Maybe their company was taking more than fifty percent.

Scrawny guy wiped his hand on his pants, then came over and stretched it out to me. I took it, and we shook.

"Sixteen hours?" he asked.

"Yeah," I said.

"We can do that."

::82::

PARTED OUT

He dropped my hand, turned to his men.

"Let's get back to work for Mr. Grimm," he said wearing a smile even while he spoke with a scowl.

I'd probably just tripled their pay for the job.

But eleven thousand for me was hardly a blip over what I stood to lose if we didn't get the ship out of there in a hurry.

··18··

I felt naked stepping out of the Fleeting Star without my weapons. Everly's clock ticked in my head, even though I was setting up options to evade that clock. I worried that I had set up too many options, that I had asked Alice for too much. When, in the course of getting the Fleeting Star ready to depart, was she supposed to figure out exactly how Everly planned to stop us?

Mickey, too, was in deep water with the schedule I had just set him. Eddy couldn't leave the ship, and despite her intelligence, I didn't think she'd be able to think deviously enough to figure out Everly's plan.

Didn't hurt to ask her to think, though.

I stopped in the middle of the gangway and flipped on my comm and pinged the Grim.

"Grimm?" Eddy asked

"Yeah, has anything come in for me?" I asked. Might as well get that out of the way first.

"Not yet," she said. "I'll ping you when..."

"I know. I was just hoping. One other thing. I want you to try and figure out what Captain Everly might do to keep the Fleeting Star from leaving dock."

"I don't know..."

"I know you don't know. But while you're sitting there on the ship, think about it."

"Wouldn't Renaldo be better at this sort of thing?"

I allowed my eyes to roll up so that I could try to peer into my brain.

Of course I should be asking Renaldo.

"Thanks, Eddy," I said. "Let me know when that comes in."

"I will," she said.

I clicked off, turned around, and went back to the Fleeting Star.

I cursed myself with each step I took for not thinking of Renaldo first. If any of my crew could think like Captain Everly, it would be Renaldo.

I commed him.

"What do you need, Grimm?" Renaldo asked.

"Where are you at?"

I reached the Fleeting Star's airlock.

"The computer bay," he said.

"Good. Stay there. I'm coming to meet you."

"What for?" he asked. "I'm right in the middle of an inventory of the software systems."

"Easier than talking about it over the comm," I said.

"Gotcha."

He understood. Important, not to be talked about over communication channels that could be hacked. I felt safe asking Eddy, because I didn't really give her any details, and she was aboard the Grim. But I wanted Renaldo to

PARTED OUT

know details. I didn't think Everly had the ability to hack our systems, which I paid a lot of money for, but the New Corbi administration likely had the capability to tap the communications aboard the Fleeting Star, and Anson Black had the access to it. If he was really working with Everly, taking chances with our communications might tip whatever hand I had.

I found Renaldo exactly where he said he was, at a desk in the computer bay, running diagnostics tests.

He turned around as I entered. The door slid shut behind me.

"So what do you need?" he asked.

"I need you to figure out how Captain Everly might sabotage our efforts to get the Fleeting Star back to the bank."

Renaldo's face straightened.

"You think he can do that?" he asked.

"I think he's going to try," I said. "I just need to know how, so we can counter it."

"You talked to him?"

"He tried to blackmail me into giving him sixty percent of our profit from this tub," I said. "Gave me twenty-four hours to think about it."

"The ship won't be ready in twenty-four," Renaldo said.

The desk chimed behind him, but he ignored it, waiting for my reaction.

"It won't be certified in twenty-four, but it will be ready."

"Well, that's easy, then. He'll try to bribe the inspectors," Renaldo said.

"I don't think so. We've already hit him in his pocketbook. I don't think he'll throw more money at it, not when he knows we could probably outspend him in the bribe department."

"He could try to hurt one of us." Renaldo kept his face straight and his voice even, though I could see the anger in his eyes. I knew he would let his rage out after it was over.

"He could. We have to be prepared for that. If I didn't need all three of you over here, I'd send you back to the ship to keep an eye on Eddy.

"But I don't think he'll resort to violence. Some of his men might, but I think he wants to stay away from being investigated by the Feds. He and the customs official here have had a few dealings that I think the Feds would look down upon. Besides, men like him don't do murder. They're leaches, not killers. He wants his enterprise to continue. Murder charges would put a damper on that."

Renaldo's fingers twitched.

"If he's upset enough..."

"He'll do something far more devious, I think, than murder. You need to think beyond the obvious. I met the man. He's a prick, but he's not stupid."

The desk chimed again.

"All right," Renaldo said. "I understand what you want. I've got to get back to this, though. If I think of anything..."

"Come and tell me in person. Don't broadcast it."

"Right."

He spun back to the desk and looked over the processes that had completed.

"We doing good in here?" I asked, changing the topic. I knew Renaldo would come up with something.

"Yeah, all the tests, so far, have run without failure."

I looked around the room for the first time. The memory array on the left hand side of the room caught my eye. There was a shelf next to it, a pair of spare memory cells, still in their shipping containers, sat near the bottom. It surprised me that they were still there at all, as easy to pick up and carry out as they were.

"Hey, are those memory cells standard?" I asked.

It would save me the headache of buying one, if they were. I could get the weapon research out of the backup data and back to where I could work on it more.

"Yeah," Renaldo said.

"You need them?"

He turned and looked at me.

"You're taking them back to the Grim?" he asked.

"We have a need," I said.

Even if I wasn't using one for a special project, we still should have had an extra one on board.

He blinked once, then went back to his testing.

"Serve yourself," he said. "We look good here, but I'm not coming back to the Grim to fetch one of them if I need it. You'll have to walk it back yourself."

"I'll take one," I said, and pulled the closest one off the shelf. "You bring the other back with you when you're done."

"Sure thing, now let me get back to work trying to figure out what that bastard is going to do," he said.

I left the room, and started back down the corridor toward the airlock.

I hadn't yet heard from Elliot, and with Everly's blackmail, I wanted to be certain my own blackmail attempt was solid. I probably had a couple hours before Elliot got back to me, since he hadn't responded yet.

I looked down at the memory cell I was holding.

A couple hours.

I could, at the least, get my research back where it belonged. Off the primary computer and out of harm's way.

••19••

t didn't work out that way. Just as I started to walk up the gangway to the Grim, Eddy messaged me.

"I need you back here," she said.

I heard an urgency in her voice that I hadn't expected—certainly not if Elliot had returned my message, and it was still too soon for that.

"I'm right outside the airlock." I walked the final few steps with care, on the off chance Everly had staked out the ship. I hadn't seen anyone, but that didn't mean they weren't there, or that they hadn't bugged it.

"Good," she said.

I palmed the lock open and stepped inside.

Once through, I hurried to the bridge, assuming she would be waiting for me there, but when I got there, it was empty.

I went to my desk and opened the comm.

"Where are you?"

"The gym," she said.

The urgency was still in her voice. I sent a command to turn on the camera in the gym.

I couldn't see her, not immediately. The light was off.

The only places on the ship without a comm camera that I could trigger remotely were the bathrooms and my employees cabins. Everywhere else was monitored, mostly because I ran with a lean crew and space is dangerous. We needed to be able to put eyes on any part of the ship in seconds.

The fact that she had turned off the lights had me worried.

"What the hell is going on in there?" I asked.

"I came down here to exercise. The lights went out, and then..."

I waited for her to continue, wondering why the lights went out.

I didn't wait long, though.

"And then what?" I asked.

"Please, just come down here."

"I'm coming," I said.

I didn't shut the comm off, but I disabled the video on my end. I wanted whatever happened in that room recorded on more than just the terminal down there, but I didn't want anyone who might be watching to see what I was doing.

I tried bringing the lights up remotely, but they didn't come up. They hadn't just been shut off. They'd been disabled, or they had failed. But they shouldn't have all failed.

Which meant that, with the threats Captain Everly had laid on me, there wasn't a chance in hell I was going down there without a weapon.

I ran off the bridge and down the corridor that lead to the weapons locker. I pulled out a pair of pistols that I liked far less than the ones Everly took from me and jammed them in the gun belt I was still wearing. I swore right then that if I ever got the chance, I was taking my own pistols back from Everly.

I shut the locker, ensured that it was locked, then made my way to the lift.

Down a deck, sweating the whole time. I swore the temperature in the ship had risen a good ten degrees since I got Eddy's message.

I used the time in the lift to check the loads in the pistols. Both were full.

When the door opened, I saw that it wasn't just the gym with its lights out. The whole damned deck was off line.

"What the hell?" I asked.

I stuck my hand out of the lift, fully expecting someone to shoot it off. If I were them, whoever it was that had done this, if indeed someone had, I'd be waiting for me right outside the lift.

But nothing happened to my hand. I retained all my fingers.

I inched my head around the door, looked down the corridor first to the left, then to the right.

The corridor was empty at least as far as the light spilling from the lift would let me see. I stepped out into the corridor. It was quieter, there, outside the lift.

The lift door shut behind me, thankful that it could finally close its maw, leaving me in sheer darkness. The doors also shut out the hiss of the air that was pumped into the lift compartment.

That's what was missing.

The lights had gone out, but so had the environmental system on the deck. Whatever had gone wrong, it had likely affected all of the systems on the deck, except for the comm system. I guessed that even the water purification had been compromised.

I waited a few moments for my eyes to adjust, hoping there might be even the smallest hint of light by which I could make my way. I pulled the flashlight out of the compartment next to the lift, but I didn't turn it on for fear of giving myself away. Like the lift hadn't done that already, but a flashlight might announce me to anyone waiting inside the gym.

I gave up waiting. I still couldn't see anything, and gave up thinking that I would. I'd have more light in deep space than I had in the corridor.

I put my arm out to feel ahead of me and took a step.

The clomp of my boot against the lightly carpeted aluminum flooring sounded loud without the hum and whoosh of the environmental systems to cover it up. They would give me away just as quickly as a flashlight.

I bent down and took them off, set them aside.

Once again, with one arm extended, the other holding a shipboard pistol that would tear through flesh but wouldn't compromise the hull of my ship, I stepped toward the gym.

My footsteps were quiet. An improvement.

It occurred to me that I should probably comm for help before I went any further, but there wasn't anyone to comm, not if I wanted the Fleeting Star to leave the station in the next twenty hours or so. And Eddy had sounded like her situation was urgent. I couldn't afford to wait any longer.

Stupid as it was, I was stuck doing it on my own.

Alice would just tell me I was rationalizing my desire to be a hero. Maybe I was.

PARTED OUT

I came to a stop about three feet from the door to the gym. It stood open, a slightly less dark void in the darkness. I listened for any sort of sound that might give away Eddy's assailant's position. I heard only the sound of my breathing.

I put my hand to the pocket where I had stowed the flashlight. It was still there.

I hesitated to draw it out.

Turning it on would blind me at this point, as much as it would blind anyone sitting in that dark room, but unless, by a stroke of luck, I pointed it right at them, they'd see where I was and have more than enough time to put a bullet or three in me.

But I'd need that flashlight to see anything. It was either the flashlight, or call out to Eddy and announce where I was.

I knew what I was doing. I was preparing for the inevitable and unforeseeable, but I was stalling at the same time. I didn't want to go in there.

And I shouldn't. I should leave the deck, seal it off, and get the others back aboard.

But I wasn't going to do that, either. Eddy needed me.

I pulled out the flashlight. Calling out would give away any surprise, not that there was much surprise. Anyone down here with Eddy would know I was coming.

But they wouldn't know when.

I hoped that would make the difference.

I slid along the last three feet of the wall, then put the hand with the flashlight out into the void of the open door. If they had night vision enhancements, they'd see me. I hoped the fist with the flashlight would look more like a blob of heat, or some other strange thing, and they'd shoot—assuming anyone was there but Eddy, and that they had any plans to shoot.

Though, I was also hoping that Everly had no plans to kill me. It wouldn't serve his purpose. He wanted credits, not a murder sentence.

I waited a few moments, but there was no reaction from within the room. My hand remained attached to my forearm, the flashlight intact.

I turned the flashlight on and waited, expecting the shot to come.

"Grimm?" Eddy asked, her voice trembling just a little.

A few more seconds passed without any other reaction.

I moved my head toward the door so that I could see through it, but I kept the flashlight out from my side, away from my body, and slightly in front. I didn't want them shooting at my face.

"Grimm? Is that you?"

I pointed the flashlight in the direction of Eddy's voice.

They had bound her to the bar hanging from the weight machine, the resistance level set high enough that it kept her feet from reaching the floor. There were remnants of tears, the silt of her makeup washed down her face, but I didn't see any glistening. Her tears had dried. She was wearing her exercise outfit, the black, skin-tight, curve-hugging suit.

She wore it every time she came down to work out, and she had an uncanny ability to catch me where she could show it off.

But she wasn't showing off this time.

I moved the beam of light away from her and played it around the rest of the room. The shadows of the treadmills and the bikes were not enough to hide anyone. The room was empty, but for Eddy.

"It's me," I said as I went to her.

I put the gun away.

"What happened?" I asked. "I told you not to let anyone in."

"I didn't let anyone in. I was exercising, and they just showed up at the door, grabbed me, and put me up here."

I set the flashlight on the floor, pointing up. The cone of light created shadows on her skin that only served to highlight the parts the light caressed.

"Did they say who they were?" I asked.

"No," she said. "They didn't say anything."

They didn't have to.

"When did they disable the power to the deck?"

"After they left," she said.

I jumped up for the bar, collided with her body, but managed to avoid crashing my face into hers. I was just heavy enough to overcome the weight they had set on the machine. It let us down, but it took long enough that I couldn't help but feel her against me where I wasn't wearing the chest armor. Her breath was hot on my face, the shadow of her lips within reach.

I thought about kissing her, then, but couldn't go through with it. With her tear-streaked makeup, I wasn't sure she was ready for that.

Then my feet hit the floor.

I pulled the bar down further, so that her feet also touched and she could move her hands.

"Grab the bar," I said. "I don't want it flying up and wrenching your arms off."

She reached up and took hold of it.

We still stood close to each other.

I moved my hands to the center of the bar, which put my elbows right in her face, but I had to keep my weight on the bar even. Then I reached over and undid the first binding. It was a simple one, used by station security for quick binding. It didn't have a lock, just a quick-release trigger that was impossible to reach while you were bound by them. Even more impossible if you were hanging from them.

I then undid the other one in the same way.

I grabbed the bar again with both hands.

"Let go," I said.

She did.

The weights lifted me up until I dangled a meter off the floor. I released my hold and fell back down. My foot kicked over the flashlight.

Eddy reached for me, put her arms around me, pulled me close. I felt her rise up on her toes, felt her breath on my face a moment before she kissed me.

I couldn't help kissing back. She tasted sweet, with a touch of desperate. Her tongue pushed at my lips, and I let it break through until my tongue tasted hers, felt its need.

And then she pushed away.

I couldn't see her face in the near dark, couldn't judge from her eyes what exactly had just happened. She didn't leave off holding me, though.

"Thank you, Grimm," she said.

We stood there for a moment, neither of us knowing what to say. I couldn't figure out why she was thanking me—if it was for the kiss, or for saving her. I didn't think I wanted to know.

PARTED OUT

So I said the stupidest thing I could think of to say.

"You didn't do this on purpose, did you?"

She pushed me away.

"I can't believe... you..."

She bent down, picked up the flashlight, and left the room.

I stood in the dark with the taste of her on my lips.

"I guess that means you didn't," I said. No one was listening.

··20··

Once I returned to the bridge, I found Eddy sitting at her desk running diagnostics. She didn't look up at me as I entered, and that was just fine.

I should have apologized, but I had other things on my mind. Chiefly, how did they get aboard, how did they shut off that deck, and what else had they done.

Tying Eddy up had been the warning, the shot across our bow. They had left another surprise down there in the dark, I was sure of it.

I sat down at my desk and looked at my comm.

A message from Renaldo waited for me with a request that I come see him as soon as I could.

I commed him, instead.

"What's up?" I asked.

"I've had some success with the project you asked me to look into."

I liked that he was being careful, but it didn't matter anymore.

"Just tell me what you discovered."

He raised an eyebrow, but after a few seconds, he did what I asked.

"I know how they're going to keep us from leaving."

"I know, too," I said.

It had become obvious to me on my trek through the darkened corridors without my flashlight.

"You do?" he asked, incredulous, it seemed, that I might have figured it out.

"Yeah. They're not going to keep the Fleeting Star from leaving. They'll stop the Grim."

"How'd you figure it out?"

"They came aboard while I was out, tied up Eddy, knocked out power and environmental to the second deck."

He fell silent for a moment. I could see his eyes through the comm as they looked up and to the left while he pondered.

"Do you have the deck powered back up?"

"No," I said. "I want you back here before we do anything."

"You suspect they left another surprise."

"I do."

"I'm almost done here," he said. "You want me to finish up first?"

I weighed the options: losing time on the repairs of the Fleeting Star versus finding, or not finding, whatever nasty surprise was down on that deck. I didn't particularly care for either option, but I'd be out money if that ship didn't fly out of here on time.

"How much longer?" I asked.

"Twenty minutes."

Whatever damage Everly had done, or was planning to do, could wait twenty minutes. He wanted me to cooperate with him. I didn't think he'd do something that would completely damage that possibility before his deadline expired.

"Finish it, then hurry back," I said.

"Just don't power that deck back up," he said, then shut off the comm.

I had no intention of doing that.

"Eddy, what are you working on?"

"Trying to figure out how they got in, Captain."

"You don't have to figure that. I know how they got in. They're salvagers. They have ways around locks that they can legally use on the ships they're salvaging. They're supposed to be interdicted against ships that they don't have a contract for, but it wouldn't surprise me that they had found a way around that."

"Then what do you want me to do, work on getting the deck back up?"

"No. Renaldo and I will handle that. I want you to recode our locks so they can't be compromised again."

"Yes, Captain," she said.

Her response was too formal. She was still angry with me.

"Are you all right?" I asked. I thought that maybe trying to be sensitive to her might help. "They didn't..."

She spun around in her chair.

"No, they didn't. Do you think I would have... if...?"

"You're angry with me," I said.

"No," she said. "I'm not angry with you. I'm angry with myself for continuing to hope that you might come around. I hear all these stories about you, about how you take every female crew member into your bed, but it's been two years and you haven't taken me. You hardly even look at me twice."

There was an intensity to her, right then, that I hadn't seen before.

"I look," I said.

"But you don't ever touch," she said, leaning forward, exposing the soft skin between her breasts. I didn't think it was intentional, not right then. She was too upset for it to be intentional.

"I..."

"From the moment you interviewed me, I knew I wanted to be on this ship, in your bed, despite the warnings I'd heard about you. I wanted the job, I wanted you."

"What warnings?" I asked.

"That you're sexist, an asshole, a slave driver, that you don't care about anyone or anything except your own pleasure and getting the job done."

"And you signed on, anyway," I said.

"Yes. I could see, during my interview, that they were mostly wrong."

"Mostly?"

She looked down at her feet, then brought her dark eyes back up to peer intensely into my own.

"I don't know why you're not interested in me. Maybe it's Mira, maybe you're still hung up on her. It doesn't matter. I'm on board this boat, because I like the job and I still have hope that I can convince you I'm worth more to you personally than just the job I can do.

"But don't," she said with a growl in her voice, "don't ever assume I would do anything to jeopardize this ship just to get you in bed."

Right then, I felt our relationship shift. I don't know how it shifted, but she had taken control for the moment, and

PARTED OUT

I knew our relationship would never be the same.

I admired her for it, for knowing that I could turn out to be the asshole she'd heard warnings about and could kick her off the ship for insubordination or whatever charge I thought to drum up.

It didn't change the fact that I still had surprisingly little interest in taking her to bed, but then, maybe she was right. Maybe I was still hung up on Mira.

"I'm sorry," I said. "It was a bad joke at the time, and I shouldn't..."

My apology was interrupted by the telltale chime of an incoming message.

I looked down at my desk.

It was Elliot.

"I have to get this," I said.

Eddy smiled at me.

"Apology accepted," she said, then spun back around in her chair.

I pursed my lips, thinking to say something in response, but my mind drew a blank.

I tapped the comm, and Elliot's voice erupted from it.

"Grimm, my friend. Have I got something interesting for you."

··21··

After listening to Elliot's report, I couldn't wait to search out Anson Black and discuss the information I had. But I had to wait.

First, for Eddy to get the locks adjusted so that Everly couldn't use the same trick again, and second, for Renaldo to come back to the ship. I wasn't leaving Eddy alone again.

I spent the time recording the data Elliot sent me onto my personal comm, and then I went through it, over and over, to make sure there weren't any mistakes or missing pieces.

The data was damning. Two dozen ships over the past four years, all of them sold for salvage to Everly via the agency of Anson Black. Every one of them was no more than two months in arrears on docking fees, and every one of them had an out-of-system owner.

Then, somehow, the salvage records were removed from the station's systems and replaced with a departure record, making the ship disappear.

How Elliot managed to dig up old, buried, and deleted records was a mystery to me—enough of a mystery that I sometimes checked the records for authenticity, but they had always checked out.

Two dozen.

I knew a few banks that would enjoy hearing about their little enterprise. For a moment, I even contemplated contacting William Baty, the erstwhile owner of the Fleeting Star to find out what story Captain Everly had told him. I suspected Everly posed as a bank official and told him that, for a small fee, if he'd just sign the papers, the whole thing could be out of his hair.

Elliot had even gone so far in his research as to dig up the arrest warrants of several of the previous owners. The banks that had attempted to prosecute them had not been able to prove anything. The defense was always that the ship had been stolen.

A couple of the owners had even cashed in insurance policies, as had the banks.

If someone, like myself, ever brought it all to light... I had visions of several multi-million credit rewards being paid to my bank account.

But I had to get the Fleeting Star and the Grim off this station. I had no idea how far the corruption reached, or what some of these people might do to prevent the news from leaking, though I had an idea what Everly would do.

I was starting to think his ultimate response might be uglier than I had imagined.

Suddenly, the idea of trying to blackmail Anson into paying for the repairs didn't seem so smart.

But what else could I do?

PARTED OUT

I could message Mira, get the Feds in on it, but I'd lose the Fleeting Star to them as evidence, and I would be out the repair money I had already spent. I could message the bank, but they might call in the Feds, and I'd be in the same boat. The bank wouldn't care so much if they had to wait out the Feds if it meant a much larger payday when they sued New Corbi Station. They'd see it as a cost of doing business.

My desk alerted me that the airlock opened, provided me with Renaldo's signature. The timing couldn't be better.

I commed Alice.

"I'm coming over," I said.

I turned the comm off and left.

I needed to talk it over with someone who could look at it more logically than I could. Any which way I looked at it, I saw doom and another uncompensated contract.

··22··

I sat in the newly re-installed captain's chair on the bridge of the Fleeting Star. The smell of hot solder and burnt insulation hung in the air, apparently overpowering the ability of the environmental system to filter it out.

The techs we had hired were neck deep in the wiring of the other desk we had to have to get the ship flying again. They, and Alice, assured me they would have it done in six hours or less.

Alice was down there with them when I took my seat. I had to wait for her to finish whatever task she was working on.

Once she finished, she came over to my side, sweating and dirty. Being a synth did not absolve her body from the need to shed heat like the rest of us.

"What's so urgent and secret that you needed to bring it to me instead of sending it via comm?"

I ran Elliot's message, data and all, through the deck so Alice could see it. I kept the sound off. She didn't need it.

After looking through it all, she said, "This is damning. I still don't know why you're here."

"How many hours are left until Everly's deadline expires? Fourteen? Fifteen?"

"About twelve," she said.

I didn't know where the time had gone. But then, they were close to being done on the bridge.

"Okay, in those twelve hours, we have to figure out how to get both of these ships off this station without losing any more money while keeping ourselves alive."

She looked thoughtful.

"You left Eddy alone again?"

Renaldo must not have informed her he was leaving.

"No. Renaldo's with her."

"What's Renaldo doing over there? I thought he was working on the computer system."

"He finished. We had an emergency on the Grim. He must have thought it was too urgent to bother telling you."

And I'd wring his neck for it after it was all over.

"You didn't tell me, first?"

If I hadn't known better, I would have said she almost sounded hurt at being left out.

"I didn't have time, and you were busy, here."

Her eyes blinked a couple times. She couldn't be angry. Synths don't get angry.

"Look," I said, "The point is that Everly was behind the emergency on the Grim. He broke past our security systems, disabled B deck, and tied Eddy up and left her there."

"And you thought I didn't need to know that?"

She did sound angry, or at least put off.

"You did need to know, just not right then. I had it handled."

PARTED OUT

"So what is your plan?" she asked.

"I had a plan, but when I saw this information, combined with Everly's easy access to the Grim, I started to think the plan might leave us a little more dead than we'd prefer."

"You were planning to use the information to blackmail them, weren't you."

"I'd hoped to get New Corbi to pay for the repairs."

"If you show this to them, they won't pay for the repairs. They'll try to find a way to bury us."

She stared at me with her golden eyes—she could keep them open for unbelievable periods of time.

Sometimes, I felt like she was the one in charge of this whole operation and that I was going to her for approval. I hated that feeling. But I wasn't about to turn down anything her intellect might produce. After all, I'd hired her to be smarter than me.

"That's why I'm here."

"You want me to help you with a new plan."

She peered down at the data on the deck, scrolled back through it.

I waited, quiet, listening to the sounds of the workers in the background. She would come up with something. I was sure of it.

She glanced up at me.

"I don't think you'll like what I have to say," she said.

"There's nothing to do but get the ships out before Everly's deadline, pay our bills, and hope for the best."

"You might be able to sell this information after we're done, but I'm not sure who would buy. Perhaps insurance companies. The banks will have written most of these ships off, already."

"And the Feds won't pay anything," I said.

I tapped the desk, wiping the information from the system. If anyone here found out we had it, we were dead.

"What are you doing, now?" she asked.

"I'm going back to the Grim to help Renaldo. We can't leave with that deck out of commission."

"What is your plan, then?"

"Get this ship buttoned up, get the Grim back online, fly them out of this place before Everly's deadline."

"He'll come after us," she said.

In that moment, I found myself smiling.

"I don't know if we'll make it off station," I said. "But if we do, and that asshole decides to follow us, I know how I'll make him pay."

I found myself hoping he came after me. Any chance to take my frustrations out on him with my own hands would just about make up for the credits he was costing me.

··23··

Deck B was as still and dark as when I had left the ship. It had grown colder, too, with no environmental to keep it heated. I walked the entire deck, looking for Renaldo, but couldn't find him.

I commed him, but he didn't respond.

I commed Eddy, and she said she had no idea where he was. She had assumed he was on B. A gnawing worry started to eat me. I began to wonder if he'd tripped whatever trap Everly's men had left behind.

I went to the nearest functioning desk and searched my way through all the working cameras in the ship.

When I did find him, he was on deck C, an electrical panel open, the wires hanging out. Just more evidence that everything seemed to be falling apart, lately. At least he was safe.

He was plugged in to the electrical console, engrossed in whatever he was working at. He may not have even heard his comm when I called him.

I left the desk and made my way to deck C.

When I got there, he still had all his attention on the panel. He didn't even react to my approach.

I tapped him on the shoulder.

"What are you doing down here?" I asked.

"Looking for the surprise," Renaldo said while his hands moved over the diagnostic computer he'd plugged into the panel.

"But they took out deck B. There's nothing in this panel that even connects to B."

"That's the trick," he said. "Take out B so we focus there, all the while, the real problem is elsewhere."

"You've checked B?"

"Yes. It's clean."

"You haven't reactivated its systems."

"I want them off until I discover what they left behind. Whatever it is might still be triggered by turning on the power or the environmental."

"Have you found anything in any of the other systems?"

"No."

"Any chance they didn't leave anything?" I asked.

For the first time since I arrived, he glanced at me.

"No."

My comm chimed.

"Grimm," Eddy said.

"Yes?"

"There's a station official at the lock," she said.

"Anson Black?" I asked.

"No. I haven't seen him before. Says his name is Hedrick."

"What's he want?"

"He wants to talk to you."

PARTED OUT

"Tell him I'm on my way," I said, and clicked off.

Renaldo was looking at me.

"Keep searching," I said.

But I didn't think he was going to find anything. A slight flutter in my chest told me that whatever Everly had planned, it wasn't just about disabling the Grim.

··24··

I met Hedrick at the airlock, going out myself, instead of letting him in. I don't know if it was a rational decision at the time, or if it was just a gut decision, but I didn't want him on board the Grim.

Hedrick dressed sharply. A dark gray suit with crisp, properly pressed lines exposed a white, slim-collared shirt underneath. He wore a razor thin mustache above his lip. His hair was no longer than the mustache.

Where Anson Black had appeared self-important, Hedrick was fully aware that he *was* important. He stood his ground when I emerged from the air-lock, though I hadn't announced myself or even told him I was coming out.

"Captain Grimm," he said.

"Mr. Hedrick," I said.

He reached into his pocket, withdrew a wallet, and flipped it open. Inside, a badge and an ident card. I knew, even before he flipped it open, what he was. One of the few professions that still carried physical idents, even though they almost always had them implanted, as well. If it weren't for the badge, I might have felt a sort of kinship with him.

"Investigator Hedrick," he said.

My heart beat a little louder in my chest.

"What can I do for you?" I asked.

"I was wondering if you might tell me the last time you saw Anson Black?"

"The customs official?"

"Yes," he said.

"I haven't seen him since he helped us get the crew of the Kestrel off of the Fleeting Star," I said. "I was about to comm him. I had a question for him."

"You've heard nothing from him?"

"No. Not in, what, eighteen hours or so? Why do you ask?"

"He didn't report in at the end of his shift," Hedrick said. "His last contact with Station Command was two hours after that operation."

"You checked the planet bound shuttles," I said, knowing he had. I said it to stall. All of a sudden, my nerve endings started feeling like my skin was creeping along my limbs.

"We did," he said. "He wasn't on them."

"What about his comm?" I asked.

"We found it on a bench near the Fleeting Star's bay."

My nerve endings arrived at full-on creep.

"Which is why you're asking me about him," I said.

"Yes."

"Have you talked with Captain Everly of the Kestrel?" I asked.

"I'm not at liberty to divulge that," he said.

Which meant he had, and Captain Everly had pointed him my direction. Things were getting worse and worse,

PARTED OUT

and Everly's entry on my shit list was moving higher and higher in the rankings.

"Well, I'm sorry, but I haven't seen him," I said.

"Please contact me if you do find him," he said.

"I will," I said.

He smiled for the first time, but it was cold and crisp as the press lines in his suit. He turned just as sharply and made his way back down the gangway.

I opened the airlock and went back inside the Grim, trying to keep any emotion off my face.

I tried to tell myself that we hadn't done anything wrong, that there was no reason he would come back here, that there was no reason for them to search the ship, but the creep had become overwhelming dread.

As soon as the lock closed, I palmed my comm.

"Renaldo," I said. "I don't think the surprise will damage the ship."

"Why not?"

"You went over every inch of deck B?" I asked.

"What I could see of it in the dark," he said.

"Get the lights turned back on up there," I said. "Our customs official has gone missing."

"You don't think..."

"Just do it."

Everly didn't have to damage my ship to keep it stuck here. He only had to get Station Security interested in it. And how better to do that than dump the dead body of a customs official on my ship?

That would be all Security would need to get a warrant to search the computer, and if they searched the computer, they would find my weapon research.

:: 121 ::

If they found that, there would be no telling what they might do, then.

"Let me know when the deck is up, and I'll come help you search," I said into the comm. "I have to take care of another problem, real quick."

"What?"

"Nothing that concerns you," I said.

I shut off the comm, disgusted with myself at the tone I had taken with him.

But time was so short, and the discussion I had with Hedrick had made me realize I hadn't slept in over eighteen hours.

I didn't have a choice, though.

I ran down the corridor to the computer bay. I had to get the weapon research off the main computer before Security came knocking with a warrant.

And maybe I could catch a quick nap while the data transferred.

··25··

Seventeen minutes with my eyes closed was all the rest I got before my comm chimed and Renaldo's voice was in my ear.

"The deck is up," he said while I was still blinking myself awake.

"Start searching. I'll be down in..." I forced my eyes open and checked the time left on the data transfer—it was almost complete. "Five minutes."

Well, perhaps a few minutes more, since I had to bury the memory module where a search of the ship wouldn't find it.

The comm clicked off from Renaldo's side. I'd have to apologize later, if he was still upset. Right then, I was too tired, and didn't have the patience. The seventeen minute nap seemed to have done more harm than good.

Three minutes later, the data transfer finished. I unplugged the memory module and wiped the data from the main computer with a secure wipe that wrote random data over the top of the wiped data. A typical security scan would never find it.

A quick trip back to my cabin to store the memory module in one of the several hidden compartments there. I'm not a smuggler, usually, but the Grim belonged to a smuggler at one point. He'd only had it for a few months before I repossessed it, then bought it from the bank, but he'd made a lot of modifications.

He was a good smuggler, but a terrible gambler.

I didn't find the compartments for seven months.

One of the compartments looked just like the others, but it had a false floor, a compartment within the compartment.

I placed the weapon data beneath that false floor and locked it up. If anyone found it on the typical customs search of a ship, I'd be surprised.

Of course, if they thought we had murdered Anson Black, the search might be quite a bit more thorough, and it wouldn't matter in that case. I thought, briefly, about having Eddy look up the local laws on murder, but decided against it. We hadn't done it, even if the evidence had been left on our ship.

But that got me thinking.

I commed Eddy as I made my way to deck B.

"Have you looked through the video from the time right before Everly's goons entered the ship to the time I arrived?" I asked.

"I did," she said.

"Did you see them?"

"Yeah, two guys," she said. "The same two guys that came into the gym."

"They weren't carrying anyone?" I asked, hoping we had a visual of it.

PARTED OUT

"No. It was just them and a briefcase of equipment that I think they used to get them past our security."

I entered the lift.

It didn't make sense. If they had planted Anson's body here, they would have had to bring it with them. They would have had to bring it up the gangway. It should be on video.

Unless...

She probably hadn't watched the entire video from the airlock cameras between the time they entered and the time they left.

I asked her if she had.

"No," she said, slowly. "I followed them from camera to camera, as best I could, until they disabled deck B."

"Watch that video," I said. "See if anyone else comes aboard between the time they enter and the time I arrive."

I didn't tell her what I was hoping she would find. I wanted her to look for anything that might have happened, not just what I expected.

"You think others came aboard?" she asked.

"Just watch the video, Eddy. Look for anything out of the ordinary. It'll be boring to watch, but don't skip even a second of it." There are tricks to avoiding cameras and other sensors. It wouldn't surprise me if Everly's men had used them. It would have been the only way they could have put Anson's body on my ship without Security seeing them drag the body up the gangway.

"Right, Grimm," she said.

The lift door opened on deck B.

Renaldo stood there, waiting for me. His face wasn't white, it could never be, but it was far more pale than I had ever seen it.

MARK FASSETT

"I've gotta go," I said to Eddy, and clicked off.
"Follow me," Renaldo said.

··26··

Renaldo led me aft, away from the gym. On this deck, there were mostly mechanical rooms and spare cabins for passengers or crew. We used the spare cabins as storage for common spare ship parts we might need on short notice when returning a repossessed starship. Usually, the rebuilds aren't as extensive as what we had to do on the Fleeting Star. If they were, I'd have more crew and a smaller bank balance.

He led me to the door of one of the cabins and palmed the door open without saying a word.

Inside, splayed out naked on the floor, was our customs officer. His skin was near white, as if he'd been drained of blood. His flab drooped off to the sides to make him look wider than when he had been standing up.

"We're screwed," Renaldo said.

It certainly looked that way.

I bent down next to the body, felt for a pulse. His skin was cold, but that didn't surprise me. He was naked, and the power to the deck had been off for hours, which had allowed it to cool.

I waited and waited with my fingers on Anson's throat until I gave up.

Dead.

I couldn't see any obvious wounds.

"What killed him?" Renaldo asked.

"That's a strange question, coming from you."

"Assassination isn't my thing," he said.

It wasn't mine, either.

"I don't know. A poison, maybe? I don't see any wounds or any blood."

"Strangled?"

"I don't think so. I'd expect to see marks on his neck, but there's nothing. It doesn't matter, right now. We just have to get him off this ship."

"How are we going to do that?" he asked.

I had ideas, none of them workable.

"We need a way to bypass the gangway cameras. I'd love to dump the body on Everly's ship and leave him to explain how it got there, but I can't see how we could do it. We've got too many other things that need to be done."

"Why not just dump him out the other airlock?" Renaldo asked.

"And have the Station spot his body before we leave? I'm not risking that."

My recurring headache exploded out of nowhere, and I had to shut my eyes. It was too much to deal with on no sleep. I wanted to curse whatever had caused me to have these headaches, but it wouldn't do any good. It never did.

And I knew how to prevent them.

I just didn't have the time.

"Headache, Grimm?" Renaldo asked.

"Yeah," I said.

"When was the last time you slept?"

"I had about seventeen minutes of sleep before I came down here."

"You should get some rest."

"You sound like Alice," I said. "You haven't had sleep, either. None of us have, except for Eddy. In any case, I don't have time for sleep. We need to get this body off the ship."

I put my hands to my head, tried to squeeze my skull back together. It didn't help, much.

"You know what?" Renaldo asked. "I'll think of something. You go sleep for a couple hours, get rid of the headache."

I opened my eyes to look at him. The light hurt the inside of my skull, but I had to see. He looked like some of his color had come back, or it was just my headache coloring him.

"You sure you can handle this?" I asked.

"Yeah, I was just a little surprised. I wish you had told me what you were expecting to find."

"I wasn't sure," I said, "and I didn't want to have any recordings of my suspicions made."

"So no calling Alice for help," he said.

"Right."

"Fine, go. If I can't think of something in the next two hours, I'll wake you up."

··27··

I lay in my bunk, staring up at the ceiling. As tired as I was, I couldn't sleep. I knew I needed to. I had to fly the Fleeting Star in a few hours, but a thought kept bugging me.

How the hell did they get Anson's body up the gangway without security noticing?

It's a space station. Cameras everywhere. Anson probably had a locator in his comm unit—which we didn't find on him, because Hedrick had already found it. Everly obviously hadn't wanted Anson's body found quickly. He had probably stripped Anson naked in case the man's clothes were bugged. Hedrick should have known that Anson was aboard my ship.

But he hadn't known anything. All he had were questions.

Like I did.

Only mine were far more disturbing.

To get Anson's body on my ship without notice, Everly had help from the station, or Everly had ways to shut down the security feeds.

After an hour of running it through my head while my headache only grew worse, I rolled out of my bunk, left my cabin and made my way to the bridge.

"Eddy," I said when I barged through the door. "Did you see Everly's men walk up the gangway on any of the cameras?"

She spun in her chair to face me.

"No," she said. "There's no shot of them in the video, anywhere. I did notice something odd with the video from the airlock cameras."

I strode over to her, pretending my headache wasn't killing me.

"Show me."

She spun back around, tapped at her desk. A moment later, video of the airlock showed on her screen. There were two cameras in the airlock. One facing the outer door, one facing the inner. The video from each was synced and combined into a single feed that gave a continuous view of the airlock as people passed through it.

She ran the video forward.

For a few seconds, it showed the empty airlock, both doors shut.

Then the outer door opened.

The video skipped.

It now showed the outer door closed, and the inner door closing.

"A jammer," I said. "They shut down the cameras before they entered."

"You think so?" she asked. "I thought they had just edited the feed. I was trying to figure out how they got into the system."

"Which is why you hadn't shown me this yet."

She looked up at me with a questioning look, afraid, I suspected, that she had upset me again.

"No, don't worry. I'm not upset," I said. "You did the right thing."

She relaxed.

"Why would they use a jammer?" she asked. "They gave themselves away when they..."

"It wasn't to hide themselves," I said. "It was to hide the package they were carrying."

I turned away from her and stared at my desk, imagining that I was peering through the structure of the ship at Anson's body.

"What were they carrying?" she asked.

His body was down there, a poison that would kill the Grim, and me, if I didn't find an antidote for it.

"I'm not going to say, at this moment," I said.

Everything said on the bridge was recorded, even in dock. I'm not a pirate. I abide by the laws. They allow me to do my job. But at times, they were damned inconvenient.

Though, I suppose, by not talking about it openly, I might have been implicating myself in the crime. Hard to know, though. Especially when I suspected the station itself of being complicit in the crime.

And as my headache raged, I came to a decision.

"I'm done with playing the game," I said.

Amazingly, the ache in my head subsided.

··28··

On my way off the bridge, I told Eddy to prep the ship to leave.

"We're leaving?"

"Yes, just as soon as Alice is back, I want you three out of here."

Whatever else happened, Everly was not getting the Grim.

Using my portable comm, I contacted Alice.

"Alice, is there any chance the inspector returned early?"

"Yes, he's on the ship right now."

One lucky break. A large wad of tension slipped from my body.

"Do you have word on Mickey's progress?"

"The inspector's looking the engines over right now."

A weight off my shoulders, as long as the inspection went well.

"I want you to meet me at the Fleeting Star's airlock in fifteen," I said.

"I'll be there."

Then I went and found Renaldo, who was just emerging from the shuttle bay, stripping off the helmet of an EV suit.

"What were you doing?" I asked.

"Taking care of our problem."

"I told you not to space him," I said.

"He's not spaced. He's just not terribly accessible from inside the ship."

"Where is he?" I asked.

"You know those EV suits we took off the Barking Lady?"

"Yeah," I said. We found a pair of suits—free of markings or serial numbers, obviously stolen, and certainly used for nefarious activity—on a ship we repossessed from a known drug runner over a year ago.

"If anyone finds our friend, they will think he was somehow trying to board our ship through the shuttle bay, got stuck, and ran out of air."

"He's clean?"

"Yes," he said. "I put one of the ship-suits from that ship on him."

"Good. At least, if they find him, they won't wonder why he was naked. He's not going to float free when we maneuver, is he?"

"He shouldn't. He wedged himself in pretty good."

Which meant we could take care of him at our leisure. We could *find* him when we wanted, like right after I exposed him, Everly, and their scam to the Feds. There wasn't any way I was going to trust anyone on New Corbi.

"Good job. Get up to the bridge and help Eddy prepare the ship. You're leaving as soon as Alice returns."

He looked at me sideways.

"You didn't sleep, did you," he said.

"Not a wink."

I turned and left.

Minutes later, I found myself in the airlock of the Fleeting Star.

Alice was there, waiting, when I arrived.

"Fill me in," I said.

"You look like hell," she said. "When was the last time you slept?"

"Just fill me in. I'll sleep once we're out of here."

"The inspections are moving ahead. As far as I can tell, the workers we hired did good work."

"Are they still here?"

"Yes, waiting on the outcome of the inspection."

"Have they been paid?"

"Half. Second half is due pending the outcome of the inspection. There's a bonus for the bridge crew if the work passes the inspection the first time."

I winced, but it was the right thing to do. It would cost more time and money if the inspection failed.

She must have caught the wince.

"They talked with the guys in engineering during a shift break," she said.

"It's all right," I said. "We have to pass the first time, or we'll be even more screwed than we are. Anything else I should know?"

"No, that's it."

"Good. I want you to head back to the Grim. I'll handle the rest of the work here. Get the Grim into space as soon as you return. Take it out far enough that you're outside the range of the station, but close enough that you can cover my ass as I leave."

"You think Everly will follow," she said.

"I know he will. I'm sure he thinks he didn't give us enough time to fix this ship, and I'm sure he thinks his little intimidation trick will work. But I'm also sure that when we leave, he'll be so angry at me for not signing his deal that he won't be able to resist following us."

"Grimm," she said. "Why don't you sign the deal to placate him, and then show the Feds the data. They won't hold you to that contract since he'll be guilty of extortion."

"I don't want to deal with the litigation," I said. "Besides, for what he did to Eddy, I'd rather end it in space."

"You want us to shoot him out of the sky."

"If he follows, and if he takes a shot first."

"You think he will?"

I smiled at her.

"I know he will," I said.

··29··

I sat in the captain's chair on the bridge of the Fleeting Star. Mickey was still down in the engine room with the inspector, buttoning up a couple items the inspector tagged. All in all, for a rush job, the crew down there had done exceptional work. The bridge work crew were paid and gone. The engine room crew waited in a break room, relaxing, should they be needed.

I tried to lean my head back, get a few minutes of peace behind closed eyelids, but I was just too anxious.

Alice was about to leave with the Grim. With any luck, Everly would follow her out. I was planning on it. The tub I was going to fly didn't have any ship to ship weapons to speak of. A pair of anti-boarding turrets was the extent of its armament.

I wasn't worried about Everly boarding us.

I was worried about him holing the ship, emptying our air into the void, and taking the ship as salvage.

I was also worried that his ship was better armed than the Grim, though that didn't always matter. In space, a lucky shot can end a battle.

If only we had one of the weapons I had been researching.

The comm chimed.

"The inspector's done," said Mickey. "You need to come down and sign off."

The timing was horrid. I wanted to be on the bridge to watch the Grim's departure. I wanted the larger screens.

Not like there was much I could do from there that I couldn't do with my portable comm if it all went wrong. If it all went wrong, there was little I could do at all.

And the inspector would want to point things out to me. They always did.

"I'm on my way," I said.

I linked my portable comm to the captain's desk. I wanted whatever data I could get out of it should the Grim depart while I was dicking with the inspector. It wouldn't be much, but it would be better than I could get from my portable comm, alone.

Then I made my way down to the engine room.

When I stepped in, Mickey and the inspector, a lanky, blonde-haired man with pockmarks on his cheeks, were leaning up against one of the engines, chatting. The inspector's deep blue Federal Transportation Commission uniform had lines as sharp as any machined edge. An indication that he was as meticulous as they came. It gave me a good feeling about the work done, if he was ready to sign off on it.

"Inspector," I said as I entered, drawing his attention.

He turned to face me, a goofy grin on his face that belied his otherwise sharp appearance.

PARTED OUT

"Captain Grimm," he said. "I've signed off on your repairs. I'll just need your signature, and then we can all get back to doing what we love best."

I wondered what that he loved doing best, but didn't bother to ask. I'd probably never see him again.

My comm chimed at me, wanting my attention. I glanced down at it and saw a message from Alice that said they had cut ties with the station and were preparing to leave.

They were exactly at the point where I thought everything might come apart. The station had to clear them for departure. If Hedrick, or anyone, suspected Anson was dead and was aboard my ship, they might deny the departure. If Everly saw the Grim was departing and notified their contact within the station administration, they might deny the departure.

I couldn't do anything for it but watch and see what transpired, but I had to take care of business on the Fleeting Star, too.

I hurried across the room to the inspector.

He held out his hand, and I took it, shook, trying to give the inspector my full attention.

I didn't want him to think I was being rude and take it out on me by finding some last minute thing that he missed. He may have signed, but until I signed, the approval wouldn't get filed in the system, and it might as well never have existed.

"I'm really sorry," I said. "I would love to go over all the details with you, but something just came up that I have to attend to. Would you mind just hitting the highlights for me?"

"Of course," he said. "I understand. I'll do my best to keep it short. After all, I've already gone over it with Mickey."

It figured that they'd be on a first name basis already.

The inspector lifted up his board, and pulled up the details of the inspection.

I pretended to look them over, but I honestly didn't care much. Mickey did the work, and the inspector signed off on it. It was good enough for me.

"There were only a few quibbles I had with the installations. Minor things, really, but as you know, in space, the minor can become major right quick."

I wondered how much time he had actually spent in space, but I nodded as if what he said were true.

"Engine number two had a stabilization core with an underperforming balance monitor. Mickey tightened that up. It's within spec, now, but I suspect the monitor will need to be replaced before long."

"Of course," I said. I wouldn't be replacing it, though.

"The power couplings for the overload regulator were loose in their sockets. They seem to have been damaged recently. Again, they're within spec, now, but I would recommend they be replaced as soon as possible."

My comm chimed again. I looked down. Alice was initiating low g undocking maneuvers. No indication from her that the Everly was responding, yet. It would probably take Everly twenty minutes, at the very least, to get his ship buttoned up and ready to depart. And he'd still have to request a departure window from Station Command. If we were lucky, they wouldn't be quick about it.

"Captain Grimm?"

I looked up. "Oh, yes, sorry. Of course I'll have that looked into."

PARTED OUT

"I understand," he said, leaning in just a little. "The life of a repossession man must be interesting."

"It certainly is right now," I said.

"Well, there's one last item that you should be aware of, and then I'll have you sign, and I'll be out of your hair."

"Hit me."

"I have some concerns about the viability of engine three. There was some corrosion in the coolant tank. Nothing I haven't seen before, and nothing that would keep you from flying, but until you can have that looked at, I'm only certifying the engines for three-quarter power."

Corrosion in the coolant system. For a moment, I thought that the inspector had been bought, that he was feeding me a line of shit. Corrosion in the coolant system was no minor thing. A coolant blowout could cause the engines to overheat, throw the core out of balance, and generate an explosion in the engine room that would kill anyone unlucky enough to be in the room at the time. It might also take out another engine, or two. With the right amount of bad luck, it would blow a hole in the hull.

I glanced over at Mickey and he nodded. He'd seen it.

Which meant the inspector wasn't lying.

"You seem concerned," said the inspector. "It is concerning, but there is not enough corrosion to indicate any serious problem at this stage. I do understand that you are slated to make one trip to return the ship to its owner, and at three-quarter power, there should be no danger. Ideally, you would have the engine rebuilt on station, but I know you're short for time."

Three-quarter power. It was better than shutting down the engine completely, but it would make hitting our deadline that much harder. I tried to suppress my annoyance. If we hadn't had to reinstall everything, we wouldn't have had to get an inspection and would have been able to run without the limiter. We could run the ship to whatever red line we wanted. But with the inspector's three-quarter power recommendation came a hard limitation set on the computer. Even if we wanted to overrun the limit, if we needed to, we couldn't.

It took everything I had at that moment to hold in the curses I wanted to hurl in Everly's direction—Anson's, too, for that matter. The two of them had put me in this position.

"No, I understand. I appreciate that you appreciate our needs."

The inspector smiled and held out his board.

I took out my ident card, swiped it over the signature reader, rubbed my thumb over the DNA scanner, and it was done.

We could leave.

I looked down at my comm. The Grim was outbound. If Everly knew, he was readying his ship for departure, or he was on his way here to do for me what he did for Anson.

I shook the inspector's hand.

"If you'll excuse me, I need to go pay the workers and ready this ship to leave."

"Have a safe trip, Mr. Grimm."

If only that were possible.

··30··

Right after I paid off the workers while wincing at the credits draining from my account, Mickey and I escorted them to the airlock and saw them off the ship.

The airlock closed behind them, the door sliding shut and locking into place with a thud, and I found myself not really believing that the work had got done in time.

I also couldn't believe that Everly wasn't at our door.

I checked my comm.

The last message from Alice said they were away, and that it didn't appear that they were being followed.

"With the way things have gone on this job," I said to Mickey, "I find it hard to believe that the Grim just got away with so little trouble."

"Maybe he's waiting for us to leave," Mickey said.

"That's not something I want to dwell on."

But I didn't have a choice. If he wasn't going to try to enter the Fleeting Star while it was still docked, and he wasn't going to follow the Grim out into space, the only other options I could see were for him to follow us, or to do nothing at all. I wasn't betting on nothing at all.

"Let's get this thing out of here."

"Do I still get my vacation?"

I looked up from my comm and saw the hope in his eyes. As big and scary as he could be, at that moment, he looked like an eager child waiting for a treat.

"Depends on how well you did your job," I said. "Three-quarter power isn't going to get this tub anywhere fast."

"I can override the limiter," he said.

"You can?"

"Sure," he said. "It's simple."

"Bypassing Federation security without getting caught is simple?"

He laughed.

"I want my vacation."

··31··

I sat at the command desk on the bridge of the Fleeting Star and contacted Station Command while Mickey started bringing up the systems, one by one, from the other functioning desk. The space where the third desk should have been was an empty hole. It didn't bother me much. I've flown ships with far greater disabilities than a missing desk.

After a few moments, a man appeared on my screen, young, but with a shapeless face and a disaffected look. The thrill of working in space had obviously worn thin.

"Freighter Fleeting Star, you have a request?" he asked.

"We're requesting a departure window," I said.

"Is your destination in system?"

They always asked.

"No. Our destination is TertiAnni," I lied.

They could figure it out, given enough time. All the paperwork that had passed through the station about the Fleeting Star indicated the bank that had repossessed it. It wasn't any secret. But you don't know who is on the other side of the connection, or who their contacts are. I wasn't ready to label Everly a pirate, but he was skirting the edge, and I wasn't about to give him, or any other pirate that might have a connection here, an advantage.

"Passengers?" asked the controller.

"None."

"Outbound cargo?"

"None."

His eyes listlessly gazed at whatever screen he was watching when he wasn't looking at me. If I'd hired him as an employee, I'd have had to fire him first, then submit myself to a psychiatric evaluation.

"Your departure window is at fourteen forty-five, and extends fifteen minutes. If you have not departed within that fifteen minutes, you will be required to abort your departure and apply for a new window. The aborted departure fee is five thousand credits. Is this acceptable to you?"

I looked at the clock. Twenty-five minutes. The failed departure fee was in no way acceptable, but there was little I could do about it.

"There's nothing earlier?" I asked.

"No sir," he said.

"It's acceptable."

Twenty-five minutes to kill, or to be killed.

"The pre-departure dock lights will turn yellow five minutes prior to your departure window. At that time, all feeds from the station must be disconnected. Failure to disconnect at that time will cost you your departure window and an additional fee of five thousand credits. All docking fees will be assessed during the disconnection procedure. Do you understand?"

"Yes," I said.

Corporate bullshit, but I understood why. They wanted to make sure ships were ready to leave when their departure windows arrived. Nice, orderly arrivals and departures were what they wanted, and a missed window screwed that all up.

"When the departure lights go green, you are free to depart. Do not disable the velocity limiters, do not deviate from the assigned departure lane, and do not arm weapons until you have left station controlled space. Failure to comply will result in a warning, followed by a ten second window to respond. If you do not respond satisfactorily within that ten second window, New Corbi Station will open fire. Do you understand?"

"Yes," I said.

Typical boilerplate, don't fuck with us, way of doing business. It kept other ships safe, and above all, it kept the station safe.

The velocity limiters were beacons that all ship computers had to follow to remain certified as space-worthy. They were unlikely to be an issue with our three-quarter power limit. We didn't have weapons, and the departure lane would only be a problem if our navigation failed.

"Thank you for your stay on New Corbi," said the operator. "Have a safe trip."

He ended the comm.

I checked the clock.

"Twenty-three minutes," I said to Mickey.

"Got it."

Twenty-three minutes of waiting, wondering what Everly was doing. Was the Vulture one of the two ships ahead of us? Would he just let us go?

I didn't think so. He had to have a plan. You don't just threaten someone like he did, dumping a dead official's body on their ship, without a plan to make that effort turn in your favor. If they'd been caught with Anson's body at any point on the way to the Grim—it was a hell of a risk he took, only to let us get away without capitalizing on that risk.

He had something in his pocket, aimed right at me and the Grim, and I couldn't see it.

I commed Alice.

"Anything?" I asked.

I had to wait about ten seconds for a response. It would only get longer as I sat there, waiting for my departure time.

"There's a freighter departing, but it's not the Kestrel," she said.

"Our departure time is eighteen forty-five. If Everly is not out next, I expect he will follow us, soon. He's not just going to let us go. Have Eddy prepare."

Mentioning readying weapons over a comm that had to route through the station was not a good idea. Most stations monitored the traffic.

"She'll be ready," Alice said.

I checked the clock. Eighteen twenty-five. Twenty minutes to go. Fifteen until disconnection.

"Keep me updated," I said.

"We'll be waiting."

I disconnected.

"How are we looking, Mickey?"

"We're all set. We could go now, if they'd let us."

I checked the clock again. Nineteen minutes left.

If only I could close my eyes and sleep.

PARTED OUT

I needed coffee. About a dozen cups.

I remembered the beverage dispenser in the small compartment off the bridge. I wondered if it still worked.

"Want some coffee?" I asked.

Mickey turned and looked at me, red, sleep deprived eyes open wide in hope. "There's coffee on this scrap heap?"

I got up and crossed the bridge to the compartment door.

"There damned well better be."

32

The coffee took far longer than it should have. Between moving piles of electronic junk out of the way and wasting time figuring out how to power it on, it took me nearly ten minutes to get two cups of lukewarm coffee that was obviously fabricated. I could only hope that it had some sort of stimulant in it, or all the work to get it would be wasted.

By the time I finished, only a couple minutes remained before we could cut our ties with the station.

I handed one of the cups of coffee to Mickey.

He lifted it to his lips and took a sip. He tasted it for a moment, swallowed, and then pronounced, "This is shit."

He took another sip.

I drank some of my own.

"It is, isn't it?"

"It'll do, though," he said. "You couldn't get it warmer?"

"No. Probably why the guy had the dispenser disabled."

A chime sounded from Mickey's desk, and faintly from my own. The yellow disconnect warning light had come on.

"Time to cut us loose," I said.

He tapped his desk and sent the command to disconnect the ship. I could feel the credits draining out of my account. Three months of docking fees, on top of everything else I'd spent over the last twenty-four hours.

The bridge was too far away from the umbilical for us to hear it disconnect, but the indicator on Mickey's desk went dark the moment it was finished.

We were on our own.

I ambled up to my desk.

There weren't any new messages from Alice. Whatever ship that had left during this last fifteen minute window had not been Everly's.

I watched the time count up to eighteen forty-five. Each second passed slower than the last. It was all going too effortlessly, too smoothly. It felt like an itch I couldn't scratch. I don't think I wanted something to go wrong, but I expected it, and to have nothing else explode in my face just set me even more on edge.

And then, the numbers rolled over and it was eighteen forty-five. The departure light went green on my desk.

We had clearance.

"Get her going, Mickey."

He turned to face me, cocked his head, raised his eyebrows and squinted.

Normally, I liked to take the ships out of dock and get them into space before I let others take over.

"You've got the helm, this time," I said.

"You sure?"

PARTED OUT

"I'm sure. I feel like Everly's got a trick for us, and if I'm focused on staying in the lane, I'll miss it."

"Your call," he said, then turned back to his desk and tapped a few keys.

The engines roared to life, imparting a slight vibration to the bridge. The screens showed the gantries and superstructure of the station shift and slide slowly away and out of view as the Fleeting Star's engines pushed us away from our mooring.

While Mickey guided us out, I kept my eyes on the readouts from the engines, especially that number three engine. If it was going to destroy itself, I had a hope that I could catch it and shut it down before it took the other engines with it and turned the ship into salvage material for real.

The numbers looked normal, and Mickey was confident enough in the engine. I trusted him far more than I trusted the inspector.

I told myself that it was just the waiting for Everly to intervene and play his hand that had me worried about the engine—and the lack of sleep. The coffee had not yet affected me.

I forced myself to look up from the engine readouts and watch our progress out of the dock.

We were nearly free of the structure. A dozen meters more before we could...

My comm chimed.

Everly.

I debated ignoring him, but after a few moments and another three chimes, I accepted the communication.

His hooked nose and greasy hair showed up on my screen.

"What do you want, Everly?"

"You surprise me, Grimm. I thought we had a deal."

"A deal? Extortion is more accurate."

"Repayment," Everly said. "Reparations for harm done to my business."

I felt the engines put out a bit more thrust. I glanced up. We were free of the station. We had a thousand kilometers of departure lane to travel, and then we would be free for true.

"Grimm Repossession Services did no harm to your business that any court would find us liable for. Your salvage order was illegal, and I have proof that you and Anson Black have a relationship. He gave you access to the Fleeting Star when he knew your order was invalid."

"Perhaps," he said. "What kind of proof can you have? Circumstantial, at best. Did you know that the man went missing?"

He knew I knew. How could I not know? Unless he somehow thought his little job aboard the Grim went unnoticed.

"I heard something to that effect," I said. I didn't want him to learn how much I knew. "A shame. I liked him."

"The word is that he was murdered."

The g increased, along with the vibration from the engines, as Mickey increased the thrust. I hoped it helped me look more surprised than I was. It wouldn't be more than a few more minutes before I was free of the station's control area.

"Murdered? Did they find his body, then?"

"Not yet," Everly said with a flat smile.

"If they haven't found his body, how can the word be that he was murdered?"

I didn't want to play his game, but I wasn't about to let on that I knew anything until I was out of the station's control space. I didn't want them ordering us back to station under threat of attack from the station's weapons. They'd have to send a ship after me if they wanted me back, and with a ship, I had a chance. I was not going to take any more of a bath on the Fleeting Star than I already had.

"Oh, I'm certain they'll find a piece of evidence or two."

Evidence that would lead right back to me and the Grim, I was sure.

I stared into the screen, and for the first time, I looked past the face at the forefront and saw the background.

He was on a ship, in a command chair. But it wasn't the beat up command chair I had seen him in on his salvage ship. This one was newer. And the wall behind him was closer, much closer, as if the bridge itself was smaller than the one on his salvage ship.

He wasn't on the Kestrel.

It took me a moment to find the button to locate the source of the transmission, but when I did, I tapped it, and the readout came out on a secondary screen.

He wasn't on station, either. He was just outside of station control, and the ship he was in wasn't the lumbering salvage ship, but a smaller escort ship, a gun ship. It would fly rings around the Fleeting Star, all the way to the gate and beyond.

I should have known a salvager like him would have other ships, other resources.

"Is something wrong, Grimm?" Everly asked.

"Wrong?" I asked. "No."

I checked the navigational screens. We had about four hundred kilometers to go before we were outside of station control, and Everly's gun ship had moved a few hundred kilometers beyond that, in between us and the gate. Still in striking range, should he wish, but not close enough to the station to worry them.

"I wouldn't be surprised if they found his body on some asshole's ship," Everly said.

I rechecked his course and his speed.

He was moving away from us, and his course would bring him within range of the Grim.

"It wouldn't surprise me if that asshole's ship was yours," I said.

He chuckled.

"You'd like that, wouldn't you. Well, it's not my ship, I can assure you."

I muted the comm, which would transmit a loop of an interpolated image of me doing nothing. Everly would know I'd muted myself, but it would keep him on the line.

"Mickey," I said. "Comm Alice. Let her know that Everly is aboard that ship."

"Aboard the frigate?" he asked.

"Yeah."

"Shit," he said.

"Yeah."

"On it."

I returned to my conversation with Everly.

"Back so soon?" he asked.

"You might as well give up on getting me to sign that contract, Everly. I'm not signing, and even if I did, there'd hardly be enough money in it to make it worth the effort. If you hadn't torn the shit out of the engines and the bridge, I might stand to make a profit."

His eyes turned hard and his shifty smile flat-lined.

PARTED OUT

"You repo men, you always make a profit," he said. "You fly around taking people's ships, and you don't even have to pay for the right. The banks pay you to do it. It's hardly even a real business."

I snorted. I couldn't help myself.

"And your business is any better? Conning people into thinking you're a representative of the bank, getting them to sign over their ship in a salvage deal and then taking it apart before the bank can track it down? You're leaving these people holding the bag and still in debt."

"I do nothing of the sort," he said. "I pay for the salvage rights to these ships. I've paid for every one of them."

"A pittance," I said. "Enough to make them think they're making out on the deal. I wish I heard the story you told to William Baty to get him to sell those bogus rights to you. It doesn't even make sense that a bank agent would pay him to take the ship off his hands."

I checked our distances. Only a couple hundred more kilometers before we were out of the departure lane, a couple hundred more until I could say what I really wanted to say, until the risk that the station might fire on us was eliminated.

"Some people aren't too bright," Everly said.

He obviously meant it as a comment on *my* mental powers.

I wondered who on the station was monitoring our conversation. Someone had to be. No matter how tight the protocols were for transmission, no matter how pinpoint the beam, something always leaked, and his beam back to us would be sweeping right past the Fleeting Star to bathe New Corbi Station.

MARK FASSETT

"You could be talking about yourself," I said, in an attempt to provoke Everly into saying something stupid.

His nostrils flared.

"Don't insult me," he said.

But he was smart. He didn't take the bait.

I checked the navigation screens. Everly had closed in on the Grim. The Grim had hardly moved, though.

What the hell is Alice doing?

I wanted her away, gone. I could afford to lose the Fleeting Star, even though it would hurt. I couldn't afford to lose the Grim.

I muted the transmission again.

"Mickey, what the hell is Alice doing? I want her through that gate."

"I don't know, Captain," he said, reverting to the formal address since we were on the bridge of a ship, even if it wasn't the Grim.

"Well, tell her to get her ass out of here."

I removed the mute.

"Muting me again? Is there something you don't want me to know?" he asked.

"It seems to be glitchy," I said while looking at our plot on the navigation display. Another few seconds and we'd be free of the lane restrictions. It was time to start making my play. "Your boys did a number on this ship. I'll be surprised if the bank doesn't sue you for damages."

"Damages? They don't have a case," he said, his voice full of bluster.

"Oh, with the information I've got on you and your partner, I'd say they have a case."

"You don't have anything," he said.

My desk chimed.

In the corner, the comm ident panel showed the New Corbi investigator, Hedrick.

My heartbeat stepped up its pace.

"What does he want?" I muttered.

I knew what he wanted, though. He wanted to talk about Anson. And if he was comming me, even after I'd left the stations control space, that meant he thought I had information pertinent to his case, which I did. I just didn't want to tell him about it.

"What did you say, Grimm?" Everly asked.

Mickey laid into the thrusters right at that moment, as much as three-quarter power would let him, pushing me back in my chair.

And then I realized that, should Hedrick be unaware of the activities of Anson and Everly, he could prove to be an ally. And if he was aware...

Dammit. Maybe he was investigating Anson. Maybe that was why he was looking for him so soon after his disappearance.

"Nothing that matters, anymore," I said. "I'm going to tell you this once, and only once. If you don't heed it, I will end you."

Everly actually laughed.

"In that bucket? You've got no weapons."

"If you even so much as take one shot at the Grim, you will spend the rest of your life wishing you hadn't."

"You can't do anything to me," he said. "In fact, if you don't sign that agreement, I'll disable the Grim, send you off to an accidental death, and then buy the salvage rights for your ship and tear her apart."

My comm rang again. Hedrick was insistent, apparently. "That'll never hold up," I said. "Everyone is watching." "Are they?" he asked.

My first confirmation that he had other connections within the station administration. His salvage business couldn't have been that lucrative, could it?

But I had the data.

I knew that it was, especially if he never had to leave the docks to salvage a ship.

Hedrick's face was still flashing on the screen. Did I dare pick it up?

I glanced at the nav screen again. Everly's frigate was almost in range of the Grim. And Alice hadn't moved even a kilometer. What the hell was she doing? I wanted to kill the call with Everly, comm Alice and yell at her to get out of there, but Mickey had already warned her. She was doing what she thought best. She probably figured that if she bugged out, I'd end up as so much space dust, but that was my ship and my livelihood.

A quick estimate of the time until Everly was in range had me thinking I had only a couple minutes to get him to back down.

"You know they aren't," Everly said. "You don't have to acknowledge it. Just sign the damned contract, comm it over, and I'll leave you to go about our business. Here, I'll even send you another copy in case you lost the last one."

The contract popped up on my screen.

"Let me look this over," I said, trying to stall.

"Your choice," he said. "But you've got about three minutes until your twenty-four hours is up. See? I'm reasonable. I won't even hold the fact you tried to leave early against you."

PARTED OUT

I muted the conversation.

"The hell you won't," I said.

Mickey turned to look at me.

"How're the engines holding up?" I asked.

"Fine," he said. "I could bypass the limiter, if you want."

"No. No point in doing that, yet. What did you tell Alice? Why is she still sitting there?"

"I told her to get out of there, like you said."

"She say anything?"

"She said she was in command over there, and she'd deal with it herself."

"Let me know if it all goes to shit," I said. "I'm going to deal with the cop that's on the comm."

Mickey gave me a stern look that told me I was being stupid even answering the comm before he turned back to his own desk.

Maybe I was being stupid, but it was my only real chance, anymore. Unless I wanted to sign that contract, and I had no real faith that Everly would live up to his end of it, even if I wanted to become a party to his crimes.

I hit the button on the desk, and Hedrick's face replaced Everly's on the primary screen.

"Investigator Hedrick," I said.

"Mike Grimm. I'm comming to inform you that you are under arrest in the disappearance of Anson Black. You are required to return to New Corbi Station, and to return any ships to dock that might have evidence of the whereabouts of Anson Black. Any delay will result in the immediate forwarding of your status as an outlaw to Federation authorities, and the impounding of any ships in your possession should you enter New Corbi space."

t took me a moment to process what Hedrick said. Arrest in the disappearance of Anson Black. Not for the murder of Anson. Which meant that Hedrick did not know Anson was dead.

"I had nothing to do with his disappearance," I said. "I told you that before."

"I have evidence that points to your involvement," he said.

"Do you have video of me or my crew abducting him?" I asked.

"I'm not at liberty to discuss the evidence until you return to the station for questioning."

"You don't have video, then. And without video, you've got nothing. Did you ever stop to think that he ran off?" I asked.

"Turn the Fleeting Star around, bring the Grim Repo back to dock, and we'll discuss it."

"Let's discuss it now," I said. "If you can convince me that one or more of my crew members were complicit in his disappearance, I'll do as you ask. Until then, I'm in Federation space and you cannot compel me to return to the station without proof that a crime has even been committed."

"Fine," Hedrick said, frustration evident in his voice, if not on his face. "We found his ident chip and his tracker in a trash bin near where the Grim was docked. There are traces of his DNA leading all the way up the gangway."

"He could have done that himself. How did you find it? He had to have destroyed the tracer if you didn't find it before you first questioned me."

"It was non-functioning when we found it," Hedrick said.

"Then how did you find it?"

Hedrick pulled his lips over to one side as he thought about whether to answer my question.

Eventually, he sighed.

"A tip."

"Anonymous?"

"Yeah," he said.

"Everly," I said. It had to be him.

"Captain Everly?"

"He's trying to frame me," I said.

"Why would he try to frame you?"

I still didn't know where Hedrick's loyalties lay, and I needed to know.

I glanced at the timer on my desk and the navigation screen. I was running out of time.

"Can I trust you?" I asked.

"I'm an Investigator," he said. "Of course you can trust me."

"No, what I mean is, can I trust you. Are you beholden to the administrators on station?"

PARTED OUT

"I work for the New Corbi Republic, not the station."

I watched him for a moment, waiting for a tick in his features that would prove to me he was lying, but I was running out of time.

"Weapons fire!" Mickey shouted.

Shit. I had run out of time.

"Who?" I asked.

"I can't tell."

"What's going on, Captain Grimm?" asked Hedrick. "What weapons fire?"

I had no time. Either I trusted him, and he helped rein in Everly, or I trusted him, and gave the powers that be on the station a heads-up and probably lost both the Grim and the Fleeting Star to Everly's weapons.

I plugged my portable comm into the desk and transferred the details of Everly's racket to Hedrick.

"I'm sending you evidence that Captain Everly and Anson Black were in business together, illegally salvaging ships for profit. I believe administrators of the station were also involved, but I don't have any proof."

Hedrick's eyes went wide.

"The weapon's fire you heard me talk about was Everly firing on the Grim Repo because I wouldn't cut him in on my profits after getting him kicked off the Fleeting Star while he attempted another illegal salvage job."

Hedrick's eyes dropped to the desk, flicked back and forth over the data that had to have been coming through on his end.

"Where did you get this?" he asked without looking up.

"I collected it during my research on the Fleeting Star."

"Why didn't you give this information to me sooner?"

"I have a window to deliver the ship to the bank. If I don't deliver it, I'll lose my shirt. I was planning to pass the information on to the Feds once I was away from New Corbi."

"Yet you're giving it to me now."

"Investigator Hedrick, could you please do something about Everly? He's attacking the Grim Repo, and he'll come after us next."

"Stay on the comm," he said, and then his head ducked out of view.

"Mickey?" I said. "Status?"

"I can't tell, Captain. There's a lot of interference out there."

"Have you heard from Alice?"

"No."

I had to sit and stare at the empty chair that Hedrick had recently occupied. I wanted to comm Alice, but I refrained. I didn't want to distract her from her primary job, which, at the moment, was keeping the Grim in one piece.

If only she had done what I asked and run.

If only Hedrick would hurry.

But if he couldn't come out and get me, I had little hope he could keep Everly from putting big holes in the Grim.

"Put what you've got on the main screen, Mickey," I said.

The screen showed various indicators, a position and vector for the Grim, and one for Everly's ship. They were circling. The ship positions glitched every once in a while, an effect of the interference. The electronics on this thing weren't designed to track ships through the electrical storms that space battles created.

I leaned back in my chair, watched, and waited for Hedrick to return. I wanted to shut my eyes to the potential disaster that I could do nothing about, but even my exhaustion couldn't overcome the anxiety that kept me watching.

"I should have just signed the damned contract," I said.

"What?" asked Mickey.

"I should have signed it, just given him the money and got us out of here. I could have worked a deal with the bank for the information I've got on him. I was just too fucking stubborn. Now I'm going to lose the Grim, probably lose this ship, and everything I've worked for."

"Come on, boss. Alice'll take out that asshole. She's got Eddy with her and that girl can out-shoot anyone that guy has aboard."

It was a nice sentiment. I found myself hoping it was true.

Minutes passed.

The two ships still circled each other.

Alice's skill and Eddy's shooting seemed to be keeping the engagement a stalemate.

I glanced at my desk. Hedrick still hadn't come back.

He couldn't really do anything, anyway.

Dammit.

"What's our distance?" I asked.

"Twenty minutes as we're going now," Mickey said.

I muted the comm. I didn't want Hedrick to hear my next words.

"Did you and Alice bring over the suits?" I asked.

Mickey turned to look at me.

"Yeah."

"Suit up," I said.

"Boss?"

"We're going to put ourselves in the middle of that mess."

"My vacation?" he asked, but I could tell he already knew the answer.

"We'll be on a permanent vacation if we lose the Grim," I said.

He got out of his seat and sighed.

"We're going to try to keep this in one piece, aren't we?" he asked.

"That's my hope," I said.

I had no illusion that we'd succeed.

··34··

When Mickey came back, Hedrick still hadn't returned to the comm, so I told Mickey to keep an eye on it and left to suit up, myself.

The suits were armored pressure suits we brought aboard most of our repos. You never knew if the owner had disabled the safety systems, and the suits would protect us against a catastrophic hull blowout. We bought them surplus from the military. In some ways, they weren't as good as cocoons, in that they wouldn't keep you from burning alive should you try atmospheric re-entry in one, but you could work in the suits, and they'd keep you alive for a time in deep space. They also had some protection from energy weapons and smaller kinetic rounds.

And if we had to ditch the ship, that's about what we'd need.

Hedrick was still gone when I returned.

"Did he make an appearance at all?"

"No," Mickey said. "Empty chair the whole time."

I sat down at the desk.

"I wonder what the hell he's doing."

I checked the screen with the display of the battle on it. They were drifting closer to the gate as Alice and Everly dodged each other's fusillades.

And then I realized what Alice's strategy was.

She couldn't outfight him. Even on the screen, it was obvious she was running against the limits of the Grim in keeping it from taking damage, and those maneuvers probably prevented Eddy from getting good shots on Everly's ship.

So she was dragging Everly closer and closer to the gate, in the hopes that Everly would forget where he was and fire a weapon in close proximity to the gate. It would be the end of Everly.

It meant, though, that she was playing a game of chicken with Everly. She'd have to stop firing before they reached the restricted zone, or risk becoming space trash herself. But once she stopped firing, Everly would be able to stop dodging.

My stomach tied itself in knots, watching. There were hours, still, before they would be within range of the gate. Anything could go wrong in that time. Alice, Eddy, and Renaldo were good, but they couldn't go forever without sleep.

I wanted to end it before she got there, though, and we wouldn't get there fast enough as we were going.

"All right, Mickey, cut us loose."

"The limiter?"

"Kill it. I want everything those drives have to give. We need to insert ourselves into that mess before they get too close to the gate."

PARTED OUT

"On it, boss."

I gave up on waiting for Hedrick, and I ended the comm. He could comm me back if he needed to, but I had to try to talk to Everly. Maybe I could distract him.

I tapped the ident for his ship and initiated the comm.

His face showed on my screen about ten seconds later. Sweat dripped down from his hairline, and his eyes were a bit wild. The battle wasn't treating him well.

"What do you want?"

"I want you to stop shooting at my ship," I said. "We'll negotiate."

"Sign the contract, and I'll stop."

He jolted sideways in my screen, an indication that his ship had just dodged something.

"I'm not going to sign the contract, and you know it. There is no chance that I'd go into business with someone who ties up my crew and leaves them to die," I said.

"Then why are you on the comm with me?"

He jolted again in his chair.

His head whipped around, and he shouted, "Watch what you're doing!"

I saw then that the only advantage he had was his ship. He hadn't expected the Grim to put up a fight without me on it, especially not against a designed fighting ship. And his crew was not that experienced in combat. Neither, it seemed, was he.

Alice's strategy would work if she judged the distance to the gate correctly. But the gate was still so far away. They'd be exhausted by then. They probably already were. We'd all been working on so little sleep. If exhaustion led her to misjudge, it would all be over. It was too risky, even for me.

"Hey, Everly," I said.

His eyes came back around to stare into the screen.

"Crew makes all the difference, doesn't it?"

"What are you talking about, Grimm?"

"If my crew were on your boat, and you were on the Grim, you'd have been dead ten minutes ago. When was the last time your crew wielded anything other than a cutting laser?"

His nostrils flared.

Maybe I could provoke him into coming after me, and then Eddy would have a clear shot up his thrusters.

The Fleeting Star's thrusters shoved me back into my chair as they pushed the Fleeting Star toward the conflict. The limiter was gone. The rumble of wide open acceleration sent tremors through the structure of the ship.

"My crew is more than a match for yours," Everly said, temporarily unaware that we had just started to accelerate toward them.

"Then why can't you kill the Grim?" I asked. "Why are you still fighting?"

"I'm not interested in killing it. I'm going to disable it, gut the crew, and take my profit from its bones."

"You had better hurry," I said. "Because I'm coming for you."

His eyes flicked away for the briefest of moments.

"In that?" he asked. "You've got no weapons."

"Don't be so sure," I said.

"I'll rip holes in that ship, too."

I looked at the nav screen.

Our acceleration would bring us within range of Everly's guns in twelve minutes. Just presenting the Fleeting

PARTED OUT

Star as a target could be enough to turn the balance in Alice's favor.

Then the emergency comm, a channel that every ship was required to listen to, broke through my chat with Everly, overriding Everly's face with Investigator Hedrick's. Hedrick's voice boomed out.

"Captain Roderick Everly, this is Investigator Hedrick of New Corbi Republic Security. You are hereby ordered to stand down and return to New Corbi station for questioning. Should you refuse to obey this order, your ships will be impounded and a bounty of a million credits for your capture will be registered with the Federation."

I split the screen so that I could continue to watch Everly. I needed to see his reaction.

Mickey's head spun around at this.

"A million credits? I hope he refuses to stand down."

Everly's voice sounded over the same emergency channel, but in the other, his pale face had gone red.

"You have no authority, Investigator Hedrick. I have been given authorization to..."

"Your authorization has been deemed fraudulent. The issuer is in custody."

So that's what Hedrick had been up to.

"You have two minutes to comply," Hedrick said.

I watched and waited, and resisted the urge to make a comment. My best hope was that he would surrender to Hedrick, and I could be on my way. My worst fear, he would blame me and take it out on the Grim.

I made sure I was muted.

"Mickey, are they still shooting?"

"As far as I can tell," he said. "There's a lot of energy

in the area. This tub's equipment makes it hard to tell what's going on."

The closer we got, the easier it would be to resolve what was happening, who was shooting at who, but we still had ten minutes.

A maneuver, I didn't know if it was evasive or aggressive, threw Everly sideways so that his head left my screen for a moment.

When he sat back up, he said, "As you can see, Investigator, I'm under attack out here."

"We are aware that you instigated the attack, Captain," Hedrick said. "Break it off. You have one minute left."

I was about to bring up Alice on a third comm when she preempted me.

"I see what you're doing, Captain," she said. Her hair was wet with sweat, her face flushed, but her eyes and voice were steady as if nothing out of the ordinary were happening. "You should exit the system."

"You can't best that ship," I said. "I can't afford to lose the Grim."

"I don't need to best it. I just need to keep him busy while you escape. I thought you would see that."

"Alice, you're leading him toward the gate. I know you're hoping to use the gate defense systems to take him out as you break off, but I don't want you risking that they'll take you out, too. The moment you stop firing, he'll stop having to dodge, and it'll be the end of the Grim."

"No it won't, Captain."

"Are you listening to the Emergency Channel?"

"Yes. He won't break off," she said.

PARTED OUT

I knew that, no matter how much I wanted to believe she was wrong. Everly was already rogue, having bilked banks and starship owners out of millions of credits, as well as murdering his partner and trying to pin the blame on us.

"I can't believe you are advocating so much risk," I said. "The cost of losing the Grim far outweighs what we'd lose on this bucket. If we lose the Grim, we're done..."

"Captain, you are not seeing the risks correctly. If we lose either ship, we lose. You need the payday for the Grim to keep flying. We sunk credits into getting that thing out of the dock and into space. If you lose the Grim, you have no ship to fly. If you lose the Fleeting Star, you have no money to pay people to fly it."

"Your time is up, Captain Everly," I heard Hedrick say through the haze of realization.

Alice was right. In my exhaustion, I had forgotten about what getting this tub out of dock had cost us. I'd only get that money back if the ship was returned to the bank.

"Goddammit Mickey," I said.

"What?"

"Peel off. Head for the gate."

"But the Grim?"

He apparently hadn't heard my conversation with Alice, or hadn't listened closely.

"Alice has a plan," I said. "If we don't get this tub back to the bank in one piece, I won't be able to pay you for this trip, let alone your vacation."

And if the Grim didn't get back, I'd have to take up another occupation, but at least I wouldn't be broke.

I stared longingly at the navigation screen, hoping Alice was right and that her tactic would work.

As Mickey altered our course and the g kicked in, I saw that Everly was pulling away from the Grim. The energy glitches cleared up.

"He's stopped firing," Alice said.

"I guess I was wrong about him," I said.

Alice blinked a couple times. Apparently she couldn't believe that she'd been wrong either.

Both of us being wrong at the same time was a first.

··35··

Mickey backed off the thrust as he altered our course. "The Feds aren't going to know you bypassed the limiter, are they?" I asked.

"No. It won't report anything except that we hit the limit."

I kept an eye on Everly's course over the next few minutes. He turned his ship around, back toward the station. I hadn't heard him acknowledge Hedrick's demands, but for all I could tell, he was complying.

Except that his course back to the station would bring him within spitting distance of the Fleeting Star.

My body suddenly decided to tense up again, the familiar headache returning to plague me.

"Hey, Mickey, keep your distance from him."

"You don't think he'd..." Mickey cut himself off, and immediately started tapping at his desk.

The g shifted as Mickey put us on a course that would give us as wide a distance as we could get in the time we had to get it. It wouldn't be enough, the range was closing too quickly, but it would give us a chance if Everly had other intentions.

"Alice," I said into the comm, "have Eddy keep her guns on that vulture."

"Already ordered," she said.

I hadn't thought she would have relaxed her guard, but it was better to be sure. As tired as we all were, mistakes could be made, even by Alice.

And I found myself thinking the two of us had just made another one.

I ran some calculations on my desk, our course, his course, anticipated range of his weapons. I ran them again because I didn't like the answer. When the answer came out the same, I tossed my empty coffee cup at the navigation screen, where it clanged off and clattered to the floor.

Mickey turned and looked at me, but kept his mouth shut. Smart.

"Give us everything those engines can give us, Mickey," I said.

"Everything?"

"Yeah. We're going to have to pass close by Everly, and I want to present as difficult a target for him to hit as we can."

The thrust cut in, pushing me back in my seat. It wasn't quite the same level of thrust the Grim could generate, and it wouldn't outrun the frigate Everly was flying around in, but the Fleeting Star was empty, and the change in g was substantial enough to give me that momentary thrill ride feel.

And it would cut the length of our exposure to Everly's weapons on the first pass to less than a minute—still an unpleasant length of time, but better than if we were cruising along at the speeds the limiter would allow us to obtain. Of course, he'd spin around and catch up but if the third engine held up long enough, we'd be close to the gate's no fire zone.

I chuckled involuntarily.

"What's so funny?" Mickey asked.

"I'm hoping we can do what I just instructed Alice not to do."

"What's that?"

"Drag Everly into range of the gate and hope the gate takes care of him."

Mickey went silent for a while, and I continued to watch the navigation screen.

Everly hadn't deviated from his course, yet. He was still heading straight back to the station.

He wouldn't have to deviate much, though, to intercept us.

Hedrick's comm flashed at me. He wanted attention. I wasn't exactly ready to give it to him, but ignoring an investigator was never a good idea.

I brought his comm to the fore.

"I'm a bit busy, at the moment," I said to him.

"I need you to bring that ship back to the station," he said. "Your other ship, too."

"Why? You're not still going to arrest me, are you?"

"No, but they are part of an investigation, and we need to send forensics teams aboard."

I glanced up at the nav screen. Everly would be in range in about thirty seconds, if my estimates of his weapon capabilities were accurate. If I was wrong, we could be in range of him right then.

"I can see why you would need the Grim, but the Fleeting Star would hardly have any evidence left. Work crews have gone throughout the ship and repaired most of the damage they did."

"There might still be clues as to Anson Black's disappearance," he said.

"Are you prepared to compensate me for my losses?" I asked.

Fifteen seconds.

I flipped through the functions on my desk, found the defensive measures. The ship had shields and a pair of countermeasure launchers. The launchers were empty. I brought up the shields. They might give us a few seconds, though I had little hope they would give us more than that.

"Your losses?"

"If I don't return this ship to Antarra First Intergalactic Bank within the next two days, I stand to lose a substantial amount of money. I need that money to cover the expenses I incurred in fixing the ship after Anson and the administration of New Corbi Station allowed Everly to start tearing apart the Fleeting Star."

Five seconds.

"I'll look into it," he said. "How much are we talking about?"

"A few million..."

The ship lurched, throwing me sideways.

"Mickey?"

"He fired on us, Captain."

The nav screen showed that Everly had changed course, and had aimed himself at us. We'd fly right by him in less than a minute, if the shields held that long.

"Captain Grimm, what's going on?" Hedrick asked.

I ignored him.

PARTED OUT

Were we hit?

I flipped through the defensive screens. The shield seemed to have taken the hit. It was down to about sixty percent. It was recharging, but the recharge was slow. Two more shots like the one we took would break them.

"Evade, Mickey," I said.

Right, like the ship could evade even another cargo ship, but we had to try.

"Captain Grimm!"

"Everly's shooting at us, Hedrick. No time to talk."

I shut off his comm, and switched to Everly's, which was, miraculously, still up, if muted. Everly wore a feral grin on his face. He was watching another part of his screen intently.

I unmuted the comm.

"What the hell are you doing, Everly?"

His gaze came back to stare into the screen. Our ships were close enough together that his response was almost instantaneous.

The Fleeting Star lurched to starboard, but it didn't feel like we'd been hit again.

"Ah, I missed you," Everly said. "Your pilot is pretty good. Let's see if he can dodge these."

"Missiles," Mickey shouted.

And the countermeasure tubes were empty.

"How many?"

"Four," he said.

Too many for the shields to take. We needed Alice.

I muted Everly's comm again, and flipped to Alice.

"Alice? Where are you?"

"I'm coming, Captain."

"We've got missiles inbound," I said.

I looked up at the nav screen. I couldn't tell if she was close enough to put a few good shots on them. She had trailed Everly, but just out of range of him. I could see they were piling on the thrust, but...

"You have countermeasures?" she asked.

"No, the tubes are empty. Probably Everly's doing."

Mickey was doing everything he could to throw the missiles off, tossing me around in my seat. But they weren't going to get thrown off, not by the decidedly sluggish Fleeting Star.

I had to think.

But my mind wasn't working.

"Turn into them," Alice said.

"What?"

"Turn into them. You'll present a smaller profile."

And there were empty cargo bays in the front.

"Mickey, turn toward the missiles," I said.

"Boss?"

"Just do it!"

I frantically tapped at my board, closing all the bulkheads that weren't already closed. Mickey threw everything he could into turning the ship toward the missiles. The g tossed me sideways, threatened to pull me out of the seat, but I kept tapping.

"As soon as we're around, seal your suit."

The shields had reached sixty-three percent. Not nearly enough to take the worst of the missiles. They might save us from two, maybe three. The fourth would get through for certain.

I checked the inbound trace.

Four seconds.

PARTED OUT

"Sad to see you go," Everly said. Apparently I hadn't muted his end. "We could have worked together, you and I, but you had to fuck me, didn't you."

Two seconds.

Mickey flipped his helmet over his head, and I did the same.

One second.

In rapid succession, the four missiles struck. The first two impacts were muted by the shields. I watched the indicator drop. Thirty-six percent, eleven percent. The third missile broke on the shield, but depleted it as well. The concussion shook the ship and multiple damage indicators on my desk suddenly lit up.

The fourth struck the hull, off center on the forward cargo bay.

The impact tossed me from my seat—tossed Mickey, too.

The lights on the bridge dimmed a little, then returned.

I climbed back in my seat.

My desk was a mess of damage indicators and other warning lights all clamoring for my attention.

The first thing I checked, while Mickey was climbing back into his own chair, was whether the bulkheads held. I had to know if we were losing air.

As far as I could tell, we were in good shape, relatively. Using the cargo bay as a buffer had kept us alive.

But now, we weren't heading for the gate. We were heading straight for Everly.

"Smart move, Grimm," said Everly. "It won't save you, you know. Just makes this more fun for me."

I unmuted the comm and routed it to Hedrick's channel so that Hedrick could listen in.

"Go to hell, Everly," I said.

"Oh, you don't have to worry about that. I know I'm on my way, and I'm fine with it. But you? I hope you're fine with it. I'm taking you with me."

The shield indicator said one percent.

We were flying in a damned target, one with a gaping hole in it.

The distance between Everly's ship and the Fleeting Star was shrinking rapidly. Maybe thirty seconds until we passed him.

I was again tempted to ram him. Our chances of surviving were far better in a collision than they were if he fired at us again. But in order to get a payout, the bank would want proof that I had done everything I could to avoid losing the ship.

Which meant we couldn't ram him.

On the nav panel, I saw that Alice had closed the difference. They were in range. She could fire, but she wasn't.

What the hell was she doing?

"What I want to know, Everly, is why you killed Anson."

"Killed Anson?" He laughed. "You think you're going to trick me into admitting I killed him. Nice try. You don't have to trick me. Since I'm going to kill you, I'll admit it. I *did* kill Anson. The little prick turned on us, put everything in jeopardy.

"It wasn't just me, though. His bosses wanted him dead. Paid me extra to do it for them."

Twenty seconds left. Everly wasn't pulling up. It looked for all the universe like he intended to ram *us*.

"You get that Hedrick?" I asked.

"I did," he said.

"Mickey, I'm taking the helm," I said.

I tapped my desk.

The controls popped up on the screen, the navigation charts, everything. The comm windows were shunted to the top. Tiny windows. Everly, flanked on one side by Alice, the other by Hedrick. He was boxed in and didn't know it.

I tried a move off to the left, and Everly's ship adjusted.

Eighteen seconds.

Everly scowled. "You're a bastard, you know that, Grimm?"

"I wasn't aware," I said.

Sixteen seconds.

I tried a move in the opposite direction.

Everly followed.

"We never had to be in this position. If you had just partnered with me..."

"I don't partner with slime," I said.

Ten seconds.

Why wasn't Alice shooting at Everly?

I could see her golden eyes in her comm window, staring intensely at something just off to her left. It looked like she was staring over my shoulder. She had to be watching her own nav screen.

Nine seconds.

Hedrick, too, looked tense. I wondered if he had a nav screen he was watching.

"Stand down, Everly," Hedrick said over the emergency channel.

Eight seconds.

"Not a chance, Investigator."

Seven seconds.

I checked the shield strength. Four percent.

Everly was cutting this close.

Four seconds.

I pushed the ship into a dive.

"Now," I heard Alice say.

Two seconds.

Everly's comm lit up with a bright blue-white lite.

The Fleeting Star shuddered and groaned underneath me.

Everly's ship lurched away from us, a big ball of plasma engulfing it.

And then he was behind us.

The light faded on his screen. His shields had taken the hit, but he hadn't been able to adjust to my maneuver.

But he did adjust his course.

We were no longer heading toward the gate. If he came around on us, there was no chance we could outrun him. I'd have to hope that the Grim would be able to take care of him.

But Everly didn't swing around to follow us. Instead, he pointed his ship toward the gate and piled on the thrust.

"You win, this time, Grimm," Everly said. "But watch your back. I'm not done with you."

"Coward," I said.

"No," he said. "Prudent. Besides, it looks like your ship has a few problems and I don't want to be anywhere near when it blows."

The Fleeting Star shuddered, again.

But nothing had hit us.

"Grimm..." Mickey said.

The engine.

··36··

I cut the thrust completely so that we were drifting in
space, but the shuddering continued.

"Shut it down, Mickey!"

"Working on it."

I brought up the engine status on my desk.

The heat levels of the third engine were all in the red.
Coolant, bypass systems, everything.

The temperature in the engine room had already risen
to two hundred degrees. It was still climbing.

Engines one and two shut off. Under normal circumstances, it would take them about an hour to cool completely.
But if the temperature in the room rose much further, it
would take much longer before their reactions were inert.

Number three was still running, though.

"It won't shut off," Mickey said, anticipating my question.

He looked at me.

We both knew what that meant.

With the coolant not cooling, if there was any even left in the lines, the reaction was out of control, and it would grow more vigorous with each passing moment.

"I thought you said it could take it," I said.

"I thought it would. I didn't anticipate we'd have to run full power for so long," he said.

Neither had I.

I checked the damage indicators on my board.

And realized our mistake.

The coolant lines ran the length of the ship, all the way up to the bow. It was a stupid design flaw. I don't know how the ship even got built. Running the coolant lines along the entire length of the ship where a single rupture could expose the ship to a catastrophic decompression. I know why they did it. It saved quite a bit of money on active cooling systems. It was still stupid, even for a freighter.

"It wasn't running full power that did it," I said.

"The coolant lines." he said, comprehending.

"That missile severed the line for number three. I missed it."

We could have shut off number three right away if I hadn't been so busy trying to stay alive.

"If we get down there, fix the line, pump some coolant into it, can we save the engine?" I asked.

"Theoretically," he said, "if the line isn't too damaged and we have enough time."

"Alice," I said, "be ready to rescue us."

"Renaldo's already in the shuttle."

"Looks like I got you, anyway," Everly said through the comm.

I jumped out of my chair and checked the nav screen

PARTED OUT

one last time. Everly was almost at the gate. Pirate in truth, now. No longer just a vulture.

His beacon winked out as his ship transitioned through the gate.

I didn't have time to curse him. I knew where he'd be, if I ever needed to find him. Out on the Fringe.

"Let's see if we can't save this piece of shit, Mickey," I said.

··37··

We picked up tools along the way. A welder, wrenches, hammers.

The final door between us and the forward cargo bay had buckled inward. It was still sealed, which was good, but it would make getting the thing open far more difficult than we had time for.

I sealed the corridor off behind us so that the only air we would lose to space would be the air in our section of the corridor, and then we tried to open the buckled door with the controls.

A warning light flashed. I overrode it.

The door opened a crack, and sucked the air in the corridor right through it. Our suits let us withstand the lowering pressure, but flying debris hit each of us more than once.

When the rush of air lessened, Mickey tried to force the door to open further, but it refused to budge.

He kicked it.

"Dammit!"

I checked my comm, which I had slaved to the captain's desk on the bridge.

The temperature in the engine room had risen another two hundred degrees.

"We don't have much time," I said.

Mickey attacked the door with a laser cutter. Metal blobbed out and fell to the floor from where the tool sliced through the door. Inch by inch, he made an incision, tracing a line that would give us just enough room to squeeze through the door.

But it was taking too long. Everything was taking too long.

The ship would become salvage material for real while we were stuck behind this door.

I had to force myself to keep my breathing steady, to keep myself from pacing back and forth. It wouldn't do any good to use up my air in worried, worthless effort.

The cutting came to an end a minute later. Mickey kicked the cut section, and it tumbled out into the cargo bay beyond.

Mickey grabbed his tools and stepped through. I followed him.

The cargo bay was a disaster.

Scorch marks from the missile's explosion covered most of the surfaces that hadn't been shredded entirely. Gantries and loading equipment had either fallen to the floor or hung out into space by tiny threads of metal. The gaping hole in the end of the ship afforded me a view of the stars beyond, when they weren't obscured by the still venting gasses.

"This way," Mickey said, turning to the right.

PARTED OUT

On the far wall, I could see where something had punctured several pipes. One of them still vented a large cloud of vapor into the room.

We stumbled through the wreckage toward the pipes.

As we reached the cloud, the floor around it grew slick with ice, formed, no doubt, by the vapor hitting the deep freeze of space.

I checked the temperature of the engine on my comm, again.

In the time since I had last checked, the temperature had risen another three hundred degrees.

Mickey worked his way up the spewing pipe, slipping with each step on the iced floor.

He was looking for the shutoff valve.

I checked the temperature again. Another twenty degrees.

"Mickey!" I shouted into the comm. "There's no time left!"

"I can fix this!" he shouted back.

He came to a stop.

"I found the shutoff. I can fix it. All we need to do is shunt the coolant from engine two into this pipe..."

"Mickey, it won't help. The engine has already started to melt down. We have to get off the ship."

"But..."

I ran, slipping on the ice more than once, over to Mickey where he was struggling with the shutoff valve.

I pulled on his arms, but couldn't get the leverage on the slick floor to affect Mickey's bulk, much.

"There's no time, Mickey! Even if you get it fixed, it's already past saving!"

He turned to look at me.

I showed him my comm, the temperature readout showing twelve hundred degrees.

His shoulders sagged. I knew he wanted to save it, he thought he could fix anything, and his disappointment was palpable, even through the vacuum, the mist, and our suits.

I pulled on him again, and he came with me this time.

We worked our way across the cargo bay toward the opening in the hull. It was slow going, though, as we had to take care to avoid the jagged metal edges the missile had created.

A long, slow vibration shook the floor beneath my feet. The final warning of an engine about to rip itself apart.

I lead Mickey out onto a spar of metal that jutted out beyond peeled back skin of the ship, a precipice over the vast emptiness of space, and searched for the shuttle.

But I couldn't find it.

"Where's Renaldo?" I asked Alice via the comm.

"He's on his way. Two minutes," she said.

"We don't have two minutes."

The vibration of the ship, an uneven tremble, threatened to break us free of the metal spar, despite the standard adhesion boots in our suits. Without the boots, neither Mickey or I would have been able to stand upright. As it was, my bones were jarring together beneath my skin.

I checked the temperature gauge again.

It showed only four dashes indicating it didn't have a reading.

The sensor had melted or failed in some way.

I caught sight of the Grim, its bulk blocking out the stars behind it as it slid into view.

The shuttle slid out from its bay toward the aft of the Grim.

PARTED OUT

The Fleeting Star shook violently.

"Jump," I said.

"What?"

I pushed Mickey.

"Jump. We don't want to be on this thing when that engine blows."

"We should be safe here," he said.

"And if the explosion causes a chain reaction through the fuel lines? If it flows through the coolant lines all the way into the cargo bay?" I asked.

He looked at me for half a second, then turned and jumped for the shuttle. I followed him.

A few minutes of floating through space, relatively, was a fine price to pay for not being tossed around in the wreckage of that cargo bay when that engine finally ruptured, or worse. The thought of coolant and flame enveloping me was not all that pleasant, either.

A flash of light against the hull of the Grim caused me to look back at the Fleeting Star.

A massive pillar of flame shot out of the top of the ship, just above the engine room. Only moments after I turned to see, the pillar extinguished itself.

But the damage wasn't close to being done.

All along the side of the ship where the coolant lines ran, hatches blew open, gasses and flame spewed forth. The destruction worked its way forward until the cargo bay we had just escaped broiled with flame for a few seconds before dissipating as the fuel burned off.

A small shock wave buffeted us, but the structure of the Fleeting Star contained most of it.

I continued to watch it wistfully as Renaldo came to pick me up. The burned out hulk was now only fit for someone like Everly to purchase and dismantle.

Everly.

That asshole.

It was easy to blame him for everything as I floated among the debris. It was easy to plot revenge.

But a part of my mind knew I had a role in my own destruction. My *get the ship or die* attitude had nearly killed me again.

I tried to admit that to myself, tried to think about what I could have done different to avoid losing everything that I lost.

But thoughts of revenge were still easier.

··38··

I didn't say a word to anyone as we docked back on New Corbi Station. I didn't even go near the bridge. I let Alice handle it all and kept to my room, to my desk, and tried to work out how I was going to keep operating the Grim Repo.

The mood among my crew was abysmal. They did their jobs, but even Renaldo could not produce a smile. Unless I could figure out how to conjure credits out of empty space, I was done.

There was no bonus from the bank this time, no retainer to pay. They'd already paid that up front. If there were mistakes made, the first was taking the contract to begin with. But not giving up on it when it was clear how much risk I was taking on...

But as I looked back, there wasn't really any time I could have cut my losses. I couldn't have known right at the first what a pirate Everly would turn out to be. I couldn't have known that half the station's administrators were in on his scam.

If only I could make the figures work out so that we could do one more job.

But that's where I'd been when I took the job—short on operating capital.

No matter how I did the numbers, I had to face the reality that I had enough credits to pay docking fees for a week and the gate fees to get us closer to the core systems so that I could sell the Grim. I didn't even have enough credits left to pay the crew.

Someone knocked on the door to my cabin.

"Come in," I said, without looking up.

"We're docked." It was Eddy.

"You could have used the comm to tell me."

"You weren't answering."

I glanced up at the top of my desk. The comm indicator blinked with unanswered messages.

"Sorry," I said.

"Are you all right?" she asked.

"Yeah, I'm fine."

I didn't want to look up, didn't want to tell her I couldn't pay her, or anyone else.

She stepped out of the doorway, let it shut behind her, then came up behind me and put her hands to my shoulders. Her fingers dug deep into my muscles. She worked them around, somehow releasing some of the tension there.

"You don't seem too happy," she said.

"Fine," I said. "I'm not."

"Why?"

I'm out of money.

I couldn't say it.

PARTED OUT

Moments stretched on while she massaged my shoulders. I hadn't had a massage like that since...

No. Don't think of her. Not now. Leave Mira in the past.

"You can tell me, Grimm," she said.

"Just a few more moments of this," I said.

"You like it? I could do better if you weren't wearing your shirt."

I sat up, turned around, breaking her contact with my shoulders. I regretted it, but I had to tell her. I couldn't let her continue while knowing what I was going to have to do.

"The problem is that I'm out of money. I can't pay you. I can't pay any of you."

She stepped back and sat on my bed, her big eyes staring at me while she thought it over.

"I'd heard Alice say something like that," she said. "You've got enough to do another job if we all stayed on without pay, right?"

"You would do that?" I asked, then I shook my head. "It doesn't matter. It wouldn't be enough."

"I'd do it. The others would, too. We all talked about it."

I blinked.

"You all talked about it?"

"Yeah. Mickey's not too happy about it, but with the way we got screwed out of this job..."

I dared to think.

I turned back to my desk and ran some figures.

If we could get off the station within a day, if the target was easy to find and wasn't too far...

No.

It couldn't be done.

I turned back to Eddy, and was about to tell her that, but the look of expectation on her face was too much.

"If you're all willing to work on spec, I'll try. But we've got to get the Grim out of this place in less than a day to give us any chance."

A smile crossed her face.

"Thanks, Grimm," she said, and stood up. "I'm going to tell the others."

She went to the door and palmed it open, then she turned back to me.

"One more thing," she said.

"What?"

"Investigator Hedrick is on the comm. He wants to talk to you."

I sighed. "What about?"

"He wouldn't say."

"All right," I said. "And Eddy?"

"Yeah?"

"Thanks for the neck rub."

She grinned. "Any time."

I turned back to the desk, and she left my cabin.

I flipped through the comm messages until I found Hedrick's. I tapped it, and his visage popped up on the screen in front of me.

"What took you so long?" Hedrick asked.

"I was doing some accounting," I said.

"You don't look like you're happy with it."

"I've had better months," I said.

"Well, I've got some news for you. Maybe it will help."

"Let me have it," I said, not really imagining anything he said would help. Now that I had work to do in looking for a suitable job, I wanted to get on it, not spend the rest of the day arguing with him about why I couldn't stay and help his investigation.

"First, we found Anson Black," he said.

My heart thumped in my chest. I'd forgotten about putting him in the shuttle bay. What had Renaldo done with him after that? If Hedrick even thought we knew about the body and hadn't told him...

"You found him?" I asked.

"We sent an investigator out to the wreck of the Fleeting Star. His body was suited up, and floating around among the wreckage."

What the hell?

"Any idea how he got out there?"

"We're still working that up, but our best guess is that Everly planted him on the Fleeting Star. Thank you, by the way, for eliciting that admission of guilt from Everly. That helped a lot."

"You're welcome. The news doesn't exactly brighten my day."

Hedrick smiled. "I suppose not. How about this, then? I've been going through the case files on each of the ships in the data that you sent to me. Several of them have rewards set out for anyone that has information leading to the arrest of the person or persons involved in the theft of their ships."

"Rewards?" My hopes grew. I'd been so busy, so tired, I hadn't even contemplated that side of it. I'd only thought about selling the data back to the banks.

"Yes. None of them are very large, but the sum amounts to a couple million credits."

A couple million. A payout that would give us all the vacation we'd planned for.

But the excitement faded quickly. I'd probably have to wait weeks or months for the payout.

"How soon until I could collect?"

"About a quarter of it is collectable immediately, the rest will have to wait for trial and conviction."

So, no vacations quite yet.

"How long will that take?"

"A few months. The evidence you gave us is solid. Some of the participants have already confessed."

"Well, that is good news," I said, sitting back in my chair. I could relax, knowing that I could pay my crew and not have to scrimp for a bottom-rung job.

"I've got one other piece of information that you might like to hear. It seems that the Kestrel is one of the missing ships. I contacted the bank that owns it, and they'd like it back, whatever its condition. I told them you were here. You might have a comm from them."

I searched through my ignored messages. Sure enough, a message from Sigma bank waited for me. Maybe the guns Everly stole from me were still aboard that ship.

"Thanks Hedrick. I appreciate it."

"Don't thank me. I'm thanking you for dumping that data on me. The New Corbi government appreciates it, too. If the Federation had discovered this before we did, the fallout, well..."

He didn't have to say any more. It could have been devastating for their economy as ship owners would refuse to allow their ships to even enter the system.

PARTED OUT

"Well, thank you, anyway. How long will you need to hold on to the Kestrel?"

"About three weeks," he said.

"Great. Now, if you don't mind, I need to get to work."

"Of course. We'll talk in a couple days. Have dinner?"

"Of course, now that I can afford it."

Hedrick laughed. "I'm buying. Bring your whole crew."

I couldn't keep the smile off my face. "They'll appreciate that."

We disconnected.

I got out of my chair, left my cabin, and jogged my way up to the bridge.

Everyone was there, sullen faced, but working.

Mickey was the first to see me.

"What's up Captain. Why are you smiling?"

"I've got some good news."

They all turned to face me.

"We've got a job, I've got money, and as soon as we get the ship buttoned up, you all get a two week vacation."

Smiles grew on the faces of everyone but Alice, who never smiled. Her golden eyes did seem to twinkle a little more, however.

"So what's it like on the surface?" Mickey asked.

"I have no idea," I said. "But it'll be nice to find out."

ABOUT THE AUTHOR

Mark Fassett lives in western Washington with his wife, children, and cats. He's a fantasy and science fiction author whose novels include *Shattered*, *Fragments*, and *Minders*. He's also written several novellas in those same genres. In the past, he had extensive experience in the mobile game business and was involved with some of the top selling titles at the time of their release, including multiple *Duke Nukem Mobile* games and *Guitar Hero World Tour Mobile*.

LEARN ABOUT NEW RELEASES

Visit http://markfassett.com/newsletter to join Mark's mailing list and get notified about his newest releases!

FIND MARK ONLINE

Blog — http://www.markfassett.com
Twitter — http://twitter.com/mark_fassett
Facebook — http://www.facebook.com/markfassett.writer
E-Mail — mark@markfassett.com

www.ingramcontent.com/pod-product-compliance
Lightning Source LLC
Chambersburg PA
CBHW020951180626
46814CB00003B/1030